THE COURTNEY'S MYSTERIES AND ADVENTURES

The Shack

Timothy William Lawrence

DEDICATION

I would like to dedicate this first novel to my most precious daughter, Courtney Anne. My wife, Vicki, and I have been extremely blessed in so many ways, but there is no doubt that our sweet, amazing daughter has been a huge blessing. We thank the Lord every day for her. She is a fabulous wife to her husband of 15 years and an awesome mother to our most beautiful granddaughter, Annalise Claire. I love you, Fred.

TABLE OF CONTENTS

ACKNOWLEDGEMENTS

I would like to thank my precious wife of 42 years for her patience, wisdom, and support. She has endured much with this bonehead throughout our years together.

The Bible says in Proverbs 27:17, "As iron sharpens iron, so one person sharpens another."

Thanks to all those who have invested their time, given me constructive comments, driven me to be the best I could be, shared their wisdom and continued to support me through the years. I'm a rich, rich man because of the relationships God has blessed me with.

INTRODUCTION

I began writing this novel in 1994. It was the first one of four to be published. My wife, Vicki, and I had been given the joy of having an amazing daughter. Her name is Courtney. When Courtney was eight years old, her best friend's name was also Courtney, hence the basis of my first four novels.

I'm not sure why I waited so long to pick up my writing again and finish this first novel. The only reason I could give is that the timing was right. I've thoroughly enjoyed putting on paper past events and memories and turning them into novels. It's been quite therapeutic and extremely enjoyable.

I have been in the music ministry and student ministry since 1972. My primary purpose and prayer for publishing my novels are to help pre-teen young people to know that they have value and purpose. That God cares about them and everything they are involved in. I want them to know that He is that personal. In fact, so personal that He gave His only Son, Jesus Christ, to die for their sins so that they might experience eternal life and also enjoy a wonderfully rewarding life while on earth.

I hope you and your pre-teen child will enjoy reading about various adventures and mysteries the two Courtneys experience. May it be an encouragement to you, as a parent, to remember the serious responsibility we have in raising our children to be Godly, respectful, polite, and helpful to others.

CHAPTER ONE: THE GANG

"Aw, come on! Quit being so scared! We're just gonna look around and see what's in here!" Courtney was actually a little scared, but curiosity always did get her into hot water, and she wanted to see inside the shack they had come upon in the woods.

Coco answered, "You think it'll be okay to go in? It might be where someone lives."

"No way! It's too run down for someone to be living here."

This time, Coco had no idea what she and her best friend, Courtney, were getting into. Courtney Lawrence and Courtney Sims had been best friends since they were five years old. To keep the confusion down to a minimum, they called Courtney Lawrence, Coco, and Courtney Sims, Courtney. They never were your run-of-the-mill children who stayed inside watching TV shows and playing video games. They were always outside riding their bikes, rollerblading the sidewalks, or exploring some new place. They seem to always be on an adventure. Now, they were twelve and full of even more inquisitiveness and, once again, about to embark on another curious adventure.

Little did they know that the old, run-down shack out in the woods behind Cocos' grandparent's house, was a hide-out for a gang in Henderson County. Well, I guess you could call them a gang. They were really just a bunch of reckless, crazy teenagers who seemed to always be looking for some trouble to get into. This location had served its purpose well for quite a while. Rumors that were going around town were dogs, cats, and even pigs had been found in various parts of the woods, mutilated and disfigured. People wondered if it might have something to do with the gang. Maybe it was part of their gang initiation process, or maybe it was just their idea of fun. There was even a rumor that some human remains had even been found, but most thought that was far-fetched speculation. In addition to those wild activities, there had been quite a few break-ins in homes and stores, even the school. A couple of fires were thought to be gang activity, as well.

Both girls had heard many of the rumors, but nonetheless, they stepped up on the front porch. They jiggled the front door handle, but the door was locked. They proceeded to see if the front window was unlocked. It was. They struggled to get it open but were finally able to get it up high enough for both to climb in. They were startled and screamed in unison as two or three birds made fluttering noises flying around in the rafters. They looked at each other and gave a nervous laugh. Inside, the shack was very dingy, with just enough light peeping through the cracks to help them see where they were stepping. The large room was permeated with a horrendous stench. Over in one of the corners was a long, sharp machete. It seemed to have some reddish stains on it. It looked like rust. On a table in the center of the room was a bowl with what looked like red Kool-Aid. As they got closer to it, they realized it was much thicker and looked like the play blood you would see at Halloween carnivals. It smelled horrible. Coco said the smell reminded her of when her mom boiled cabbage, but much worse.

Driven by their curiosity, they continued to investigate the other rooms and closets that surrounded the large room. Coco was just about to open the door of one of the closets when they heard some voices outside. They ran to the window and saw about six or seven teenage boys about fifty yards away walking towards the house.

Courtney said, "Let's get out of here!"

"Sure, and where do you suggest we go?" Coco said with sarcasm. "We don't have time to climb out the side windows."

"Okay, Courtney answered, but we can't stay in here!"

They both stood dead in their tracks.

Coco said, "Look over there by the back corner. Let's get behind that!"

Leaning against the wall in the corner was a tall piece of plywood. They ran over and slid behind it just as the front door opened. The old shack had no electricity running to it, which was fortunate for the Courtneys. They stood motionless, hoping they wouldn't be seen.

As the boys came in, they were laughing, shoving, and taunting each other.

One immediately said, "Gosh, it stinks in here!" Another one said, "Yeah, smells like your underarms!"

"Aw, shut up. It smells like your breath," he returned. Being behind the plywood panel, neither Courtneys could see anything, nor did they dare try. They both whispered a prayer that they wouldn't be seen.

One of the boys yelled out to one of the others, "Hey, don't drink it all up; give me some."

Another chimed in with the same sentiment. Then, there was a crash of glass breaking and slamming against the piece of plywood where the Courtneys were hiding. Someone must have thrown an empty beer bottle against the plywood. The girls quickly put their hands over their mouths to keep from screaming.

One of the boys, apparently the leader, hollered, "I don't want anybody doing anymore drinking until we are through with this job! It's the most important one yet. Do you hear me?"

All the other boys looked at the leader and said at different times. "Yeah, yeah, okay, Max!"

Max went on to say that they all had to be their sharpest if they were going to stay in this gang. Max began going over details of a robbery that they were planning about the house across from the woods next to the golf course. He said it was a 2-story house and had to have plenty of expensive items for them to steal. Coco was so scared that it didn't register with her that he was talking about her grandparent's house.

Max was right in the middle of explaining the details when one of the boys interrupted.

"Hey, who left this window open?"

No one admitted to the crime, and as Max went over to shut it, he told the boys to look around and see if they could find anything suspicious. The Courtneys didn't know what to do. Behind the plywood would have been one of the most obvious places for anyone to look. Then, suddenly, Max shushed everyone and whispered.

"Shh, listen! Someone's out there! He's headed toward the shack. He's probably a hunter. Climb out the side windows, and I'll get in touch about when and where we'll meet and finish our plans."

The hunter didn't notice any of the teenagers because he had heard a rustling behind him and thought it might be a deer. Once he turned back around, the boys had just enough time to climb out both side windows without being seen. As the last boy stepped over the windowsill, he caught a glimpse of some movement. Courtney had shuffled her feet, and he spotted her. She didn't know if it was enough for him to recognize her in public, but she knew he saw her.

The hunter walked up to the old shack and was whistling a familiar tune. It was a chorus they occasionally sang in church. It was 'Amazing Love'. The Courtneys still hadn't seen anything or anyone since they had been standing behind the plywood. Given any other circumstances, they would have probably come out, looking for help, and introduced themselves to the man who had come in, but they didn't know who he was and why he was there either. Better to be safe than sorry, they thought! When he came in, he let out a "Phew-whew!" The frightening moments had caused the girls to forget the rotten smell that pervaded the house. Hearing him and his outward comment about the foul odor reminded them about it. He turned around and opened the door back up to get some ventilation. They could see flashes of what they thought was probably his flashlight. He took a short look around the room but didn't see anything to cause him to do any more investigation.

At one point during his inspection, he stopped at the piece of plywood and smelled the liquid that had been spilled when the bottle was thrown against it.

"Hmmm, liquor!" the man said.

The Courtneys were ready to push the piece of plywood on top of whoever was on the other side if need be, but then he walked away. He was about to leave when he noticed a bowl on the table in the middle of the room. He walked back to the table and shined the bowl with his light. After examining it, he realized the liquid seemed to be some kind of animal blood.

He let out a soft, "What the heck?"

The Courtneys stood as quietly as they knew how wondering what he was doing. After that, the Courtneys heard the door shut and heard him walking off the porch into the woods. They both peered around each side of the plywood and saw that it was safe to come out.

Courtney spoke. "I'm getting out of here! I don't care if you're coming or not!"

Coco said, "Okay, okay, but wait. Look! The bowl is gone!"

Courtney looked around and saw that the machete was gone, too. They both agreed, it was time to quit playing detective and get back to Coco's grandparent's house.

Summertime! There's nothing like it! And that's exactly how the Courtneys felt. They loved the Summer because it meant spending just about every day together. They would always ride their bikes, swim, go hiking, cook, play various video games, explore in the woods, anything that was fun. And this Summer was like no other. At least two weeks out of the Summer, Courtney's parents would allow her to spend it at Coco's grandparents' house. Coco loved her grandparents. She thought they were the best in the whole world. From the time she was old enough to talk, she couldn't say granddad. Instead, she'd call him 'Lanlad'. He was a gentle, kind man and was only 5' 8" in stature, but when he spoke, everyone listened because he always gave much thought to the issue being discussed. No one knows how Coco's grandmother got the name 'Nannie,' but it had been that way ever since Coco was little. She was a marvelous cook and used that talent to help the needy. In fact, she was the chairperson of the committee at their church that would help those who were in need of food. Courtney Sims was like a part of the family, and she was just as comfortable calling them Lanlad and Nannie, too.

They had had quite an exhausting day and were getting ready to go to sleep when Courtney said, "I think he saw me!" "What?" Coco asked.

"I think one of the boys saw me!"

"Which one?"

"The last one to go out the window."

"Are you sure?"

"Yeah, I think so. I kind of moved my feet to get away from the window, and he turned and looked my way. Maybe it was too dark behind the plywood, you think?"

"I don't know, but let's try not to worry about it now and get some sleep. We've got some work to do tomorrow."

"What do you mean, work?"

"We've got some more investigating to do. We need to find out who those boys were and what they are up to. Did you hear them mention the leader's name? What was it again?"

Courtney answered, "I'm not sure, but I think I heard one of them call one of them Max?"

"Yeah, that was it! Max! Hmmm, I know a Max, but, nah, it couldn't be him. He runs the convenience store across from the playground. He seems very courteous and polite when people come into the store. He'd never be involved with a bunch of hoodlums like we heard today. Well, come on. Let's try and get some sleep. Good night!"

Courtney asked, "Aren't you forgettin somethin?"

"What?"

"To pray!"

"Oh, yeah! I guess all the excitement made me forget." As they normally did every night when they were together, they would pray with a list they had made a few months earlier. They had gone to one of the summer's student activities called "Saturday Funday." They were always so much fun! They would have all kinds of games, relays, and sometimes even inflatable interactive games. And there were always the best goodies to eat. After everyone had played, they all gathered to eat the refreshments. That's when the children's minister quieted them down and shared with them some practical ways to make their prayer time with the Lord more interesting and real in their lives. She challenged all the children to consider making a list of things they could pray for each day. The Courtneys liked the idea and decided to give it a try. Both had kept each other honest about doing it ever since that day. They both got quiet and had their own time alone with God. After going through their own lists and prayer time, it seemed to calm them down after the exciting day they had experienced and gave them the peace that they desperately needed. They both wished each other a good night and got a good night's sleep.

The Courtney's got up earlier than usual the next morning. They weren't sure what they were going to do, but they were definitely on a mission. They were going to find out who those boys were and what they were up to.

Courtney looked at Coco and said, "I was gonna mention something to you last night, but I heard you snoring?"

"I don't snore!"

"Well, there must have been a freight train that came through last night, or maybe it was one of the nearby cows, or maybe it was..."

"Very funny. All I know is, I DON'T SNORE!!"

"Well, Ms. Denial, anyway, I was gonna ask you what house you think that this Max guy was talking about."

"What house are you talking about?"

"Didn't you hear him? He said something about a house across the woods next to the golf course."

"So, what's the big deal? Wait a minute. I know what you're saying, but that could mean any one of the houses over here."

"Yeah, but there are only three that are actually next to the golf course, and that are 2-story."

Coco sternly looked at Courtney and said, "Stop it, Courtney. You're scaring me! I don't like the thought that Max might have been talking about my grandparent's house."

"I didn't mean to scare you, Courtney; it's just that this house is one of the ones he could have been talking about."

"Yeah, I guess you're right."

Courtney continued, "Maybe we should go to the police and talk to them about what we saw yesterday."

"Yeah! Remember the policeman that came to your grandparent's church last week and talked about how destructive illegal drugs and alcohol abuse can be? I remember his name because of Moses in the Bible. It was Police Chief Moses."

"Yeah," Courtney replied. "He seemed to be all business but seemed to be someone we could talk to. Maybe he could help us!"

On their way to the police department, they dropped into Ice Cream Charlie's. It was a quaint little shop in a shopping center off Main Street. Many locals would come there and sit at the counter or at the tables and enjoy their favorite flavored ice cream. Charlie, the owner, was a kind, gentle soul, a little pudgy around the middle and always sporting his round wire-rimmed glasses, but one of the nicest people you would ever want to meet. You would never catch him wearing any other apron than the one his wife, Betsy, of 46 years, gave to him. It read, "Ice cream, you scream, we all scream for ice cream." She went home to be with Jesus about three years ago.

The Courtneys always ordered the chocolate fudge brownie with extra chocolate syrup, their favorite. And in their mind, Charlie served the best chocolate fudge brownie ice cream in the world. Maybe part of the reason was that Charlie would always give them a little extra in their cups. They wiped out two large scoops in seven minutes flat, breaking their old record of seven minutes and fourteen seconds. They both got brain freeze. They paid Charlie and went outside. As they rode their bikes down the street, they would always look at their reflections in the store windows. Normally, they would be oblivious to the vehicles passing by, but the car full of teenagers coming toward them had an obnoxiously loud, driving beat coming from their radio, rattling the street signs. They both glanced up, and that's when Courtney noticed one of the boys rubber-necking and giving her the stare of her life. She immediately knew who it was. It was the boy who saw her in the shack. She rode right into a group of trash cans sitting on the curb to be picked up by the garbage collectors. Coco turned around, and when she saw Courtney wasn't hurt, she let out a huge, boisterous laugh. As she got closer, she noticed she was crying.

"Are you hurt?"

"No!"

"Then why are you crying?"

"I'm scared!"

"Scared! About what?"

"That car that just passed by is the same boys that were at the shack yesterday."

"What makes you think that?"

"Cause I'm not stupid! I saw the one who saw me that day. He was breaking his neck out of the window to get a good look at me!"

"Are you sure?"

"Yeah, and he knows what I look like, and I know he recognized me."

Coco squealed, "We gotta get out of here. The car is turning around and is headed back this way. Let's get out of here."

Both of them jumped on their bikes and took off. Luckily, there was an alley close by that they rode down. The car full of boys saw them turn into it and slammed on their brakes. A couple of them jumped out and started chasing them down the alley. Fortunately for the Courtneys, one slipped as he was trying to turn and tripped up the other one. Both fell flat on their rumps. They got back up and took off running after them again. The rest of the carload drove around the block to see if they could cut the Courtneys off. The Courtneys were pedaling as fast as their legs would go. The alley came out on the other side, and so was the car with the teenagers.

"Come on!" Coco yelled. "Let's turn around!"

They turned their bikes around and headed in the other direction. The other boys jumped out of the car and took off running after them. The Courtneys had their mountain bikes going faster than they'd ever had them before. Then they spotted the first two boys who had been chasing them from the other way.

Courtney looked at Coco and screamed, "Now what do we do, Sherlock?"

"I don't know about you, but I ain't stoppin' for nobody. If those two have any sense at all, they'll get out of my way."

Well, apparently, they didn't have any sense. They stood right in their direction and tried to stop both of them. Once again, if you were close enough to each one of their lips, you would have heard them both whispering a prayer that the Lord would protect them. They stood up on their bikes and gave it all they had. Boom! Not only had they hit the boys standing in their way, but Coco knocked one into a stack of boxes, and Courtney flipped the other into a group of fifty-gallon drums. They felt like one of the adventure movies they had watched recently, except this wasn't a movie, and they were very afraid. The movie they had seen ended with a perfect ending. They didn't know how this episode would end!

They rushed home to Coco's grandparent's house, ran inside, went up to their room, and shut the door. Luckily, Courtney's grandparents weren't home, or they would have surely been upstairs to see what all the commotion was about. It took them about fifteen minutes to finally calm down and stop their heavy, labored breathing.

Coco started the conversation with, "I can't believe what just happened!"

"I know, I can't believe it either! What are we going to do?"

Coco thought for a moment and then replied, "I don't know. I'm almost too scared to go to the police station now. Wait a minute! Why don't we call Chief Moses? That way, we won't have to take the risk of being seen again by those boys."

Coco looked the number up in the phone book and began dialing. After the first ring, it was answered.

"Police station, Desk Sergeant Harmon speaking," Coco asked if Police Chief Moses was in.

"Sure, let me get him."

The Desk Sergeant called Chief Moses on his intercom and told him there was a young girl on the line. The chief thanked him and picked up the line.

"Hello. This is Police Chief Moses."

A little nervous and not knowing how to start, Coco began. "Chief Moses, this is Courtney Lawrence."

"Yes, how may I help you?"

"Well, you don't know me, but you came to our church a week ago and gave a speech about how harmful illegal drugs and alcohol abuse can be. It was very informative."

"Thank you, Ms. Lawrence. I appreciate the compliment, but I'm a little busy right now. Is there something I can help you with?"

"Well, I don't really know where to start. I guess I should start with what happened yesterday with me and my best friend. You see, we were just walking around in the woods, and we came upon this..."

The Police Chief interrupted Coco. "Ms. Lawrence, can you hold on just a minute? We are receiving an all-points bulletin, right now, and I need to hear what it's about."

"Oh, yes, sir,"

Courtney asked what was happening, and Coco told her. Chief Moses came back on the line and apologized to Coco that he had to go. A bank had just been robbed. She hung up and told Courtney.

Courtney said, "This is the second time we've tried to get to Chief Moses and tell him about our situation. Those crazy boys kept us from getting to the police station, and now we can't talk to the Chief because he has to handle a bank robbery. Maybe we just should give up on this?"

"No!" Coco said. I'm afraid for my grandparents and what those boys have planned. Maybe I should tell them what has been going on, but I don't want them to get scared and worry."

A rare occasion, but neither one of the Courtneys said anything for a couple of minutes.

Then suddenly, Coco shot up like a rocket and said, "I've got it!" Courtney gave her that look.

"Oh, no! Not one of these hair-brain schemes of yours."

Immediately, Coco knew what she was thinking and said, "Yeah, it's kinda crazy, but it might give us some answers that we're looking for!"

CHAPTER TWO: NANNIE AND LANLAD

Courtney wasn't sure about Coco's idea, but it might work. They both had read the same novel for a book report this last school year entitled 'Maggie, the Teenage Sleuth'. It was about a teenage girl who loved mysteries and was always on a thrilling adventure. This particular book was about two very mysterious men who were involved in an undercover secret organization. Maggie would sometimes get into serious and dangerous situations that got very problematic. That book was what created such an interest in the girls, discovering various mysteries whenever they were together. However, they never had one that was as scary as the one they were involved in now. The novel was where Coco came up with this crazy idea. In the book, Maggie needed some answers about a situation but didn't want her parents to worry about her, so one evening, while they were in the living room, she began asking them vague questions about something similar that she was dealing with, not the actual issue. The Courtneys decided to try the same thing because it worked in the novel. They would find a time when they would be with Coco's grandparents and ask them random questions, hopefully without them getting curious. They didn't want to tip them off, so they acted as nonchalantly as they knew how.

After eating a scrumptious dinner of mac and cheese, fried chicken, and green beans, which weren't their favorite item that night, they sat down and first watched some TV shows. When they felt the time was right, they started with the questions.

Courtney asked Lanlad, "Hey, Lanlad? Were you born here in Altonville, AL?"

"No, ma'am. I was born in..."

Coco yelled out, "New York, right, Lanlad?"

"That's correct, sweetheart. Albany, New York."

Courtney blurted out, "Were there teenage gangs there?"

Coco gave her a stern look as if to say, "Why would you ask that?"

"Well, that's a very curious question. Why do you ask that?"

Courtney stammered, "Oh, uh, uh, I'd heard someone talking about the possibility of a gang here in Altonville."

"Hmmm, well, I guess there could be one or two here in this small community, but it's not likely. Surely not any real dangerous ones. We had some gangs in Albany, but they weren't really what I would call dangerous. Surely not as dangerous as I've heard and read about in cities like Chicago, Los Angeles, Detroit, or even New York City. There were some very dangerous gangs in those cities, and still are. They have been around for quite a few years."

Coco chimed in, "So, Lanlad, were you ever involved in a gang."

Lanlad let out a small, little chuckle and replied, "If you called the "Blueberry boys" a gang."

Both Courtney spoke in unison. "What?"

"Well, that was what a bunch of us boys called our little group because we would occasionally go up to ole man Fisher's house and pick some of his blueberries. We thought we were getting away with something pretty terrible, and we just knew if ole man Fisher ever caught us, he would call the police or at least get hold of our parents. He was about six foot six and looked like an NFL linebacker.

The story was that he had been a widower for about ten years and was mean as a cuss. We didn't think he knew anything about our blueberry robberies until one day, we were picking a bunch, and he snuck up real close and yelled at us. He acted all mad and angry, saying he was going to call our parents and the police and tell them about us stealing all his blueberries. We wanted to run but he was blocking the way we always came in and holding his hands around a huge pitchfork with two strong grips. He could tell by the look on our faces how terrified we were, and suddenly, he let out this billowing laugh. We didn't know what to think.

"You boys are something else! All this time you've been thinking that you've been stealing my blueberries without me knowing, and I've been knowing about it ever since the first time."

The looks on our faces had to be priceless. Still scared and now with quizzical looks, he continued.

"Boys, y'all are always welcome to come and get as many blueberries as you want. I hope you enjoy 'em."

We couldn't believe what had just happened, but over time, we found that ole man Fisher had gotten a pretty bad reputation when, actually, he was one of the finest people in this community. He was a veteran of two wars, WWII and the Korean War, and then worked at the cotton mill for fifty-five years. It was a real treat getting to know him. Well, sorry, I didn't mean to go on and on about all that."

"That's alright. Coco said to Lanlad. It was actually a very interesting story."

"Yeah! Courtney agreed and then asked Lanlad, what would you have done if there was a gang that you knew had done something really bad?"

"I guess we would have told the authorities and let them handle the situation."

Courtney was about to ask another question, but Coco elbowed her in the side. With a slight "humph," Courtney slid away from her reach and asked another question.

"What if you weren't sure what the gang was doing, but you had some information that might help the police? What would you have done then?"

Nannie stood up to go into the kitchen and interjected her thoughts. "Knowing how I was back then, I probably would have done some investigating myself. I wouldn't want myself looking silly if I ended up being wrong about what I thought about the activity in question. Not very smart, though. When you're young and inexperienced, it's always best to get the local authorities involved, as Lanlad said. They've had much more experience handling issues like gangs and gang activity. By the way. You two are asking quite a few amusing questions. What brought all this about?"

Coco quickly replied, "Oh, nothing really. When we heard someone talking about the possibility of a gang here in Altonville, I guess it got Courtney, and I think. You know how we are always asking questions about stuff!"

After all the questions, the Courtneys said they were going up to their bedroom and going to bed. Both told them good night and that they would see them in the morning.

Once upstairs and in their room, Coco looked hard at Courtney and said, "Didn't you get the hint when I elbowed you in the side that you were asking too many curious questions?"

"Yeah," Courtney answered, but I figured I'd gone that far. I might as well go further."

"Well, I hope they don't suspect anything, and you know, Nannie and Lanlad were right. We really need to get the authorities involved on this stuff we know about."

"Well, we tried," Courtney reminded Coco. "We called to speak to Police Chief Moses, but if you remember, he wasn't even interested in hearing what we had to say."

"Well, actually, he had to go because of that bank robbery situation."

"Yeah, you're right. I know one thing. I sure am sleepy."

"Yeah, me, too," Coco replied.

They both brushed their teeth, put on their pajamas, and slipped into their beds. Both said their usual "Good night."

"Oh, wait," Coco said. "We almost forgot again."

"Yep," Courtney countered. "Let's get out our lists and pray."

And that's what they did and, shortly thereafter fell fast asleep.

"What do you think about all those questions tonight, Nannie?" Lanlad wondered.

"Oh, you know how young girls can be. Probably just letting their imaginations run wild. I remember when I was twelve, I'd watched a movie about a gangster getting his hand cut off in a car accident. The rest of the movie was about that hand crawling around by itself and doing all kinds of bad things. My imagination went crazy. Couldn't sleep for hours."

"I could see how that would shake anyone up! Yeah, you're probably right. Just their imaginations running wild."

"Well, of course, I'm right! Aren't I always?"

Lanlad gave her that look and then said, "Okay, Miss Know-It-All, what do you say we go to bed, too?"

As they walked upstairs to their bedroom, Nannie was in front of Lanlad.

He reached up and, squeezed Nannie's ankle and spoke. "The hand's gotcha!"

Nannie held in a quiet scream and hit Lanlad's arm, and almost knocked him back down the stairs. He couldn't help but chuckle a little louder than he meant to.

The girls heard them and yelled out, "Hey, we're trying to get some sleep. We can't do that with all the ruckus."

At that, all four of them laughed out loud for a minute and told each other 'Good night'. The next day, the girls had to help Lanlad do some yard work. They always enjoyed it because it usually meant they'd get to ride in the back of his pickup with a load of branches or grass cuttings. He'd always take them to the edge of the nearby field and burn them. Lanlad taught them to never use gasoline and never burn anything on a windy day and especially, never start a fire unless he was with them. He told them a story of one time when he started a fire, and it was quite windy, but he thought he'd be able to control it. Sparks started jumping into the nearby field, and it caught on fire. Within ten to fifteen minutes, the whole field was ablaze. Nannie was putting up clothes out on the line and saw what was happening. She ran inside and called 911, and the fire department came out. Before it was all done, two and a half acres had burned up.

They all had a wonderful lunch that Nannie had prepared, and then the girls jumped on their bikes and rode to town. They couldn't help wondering if they would run into their 'friends' again. They would make sure to be a lot more careful this time. They went to the convenience store where Max worked and, once inside, acted as naturally as they could. They didn't want to look too conspicuous. Max was a terrific worker. There were plaques on the wall showing him as the store's top employee for the past few months. The Courtneys, though, wasn't taking anything for granted. They were going to check every lead they had and be very careful doing so. They heard Max tell one of the other employees that he would be off in another fifteen minutes. What luck! Enough time for them to get to their bikes and discreetly follow Max. Standing beside their mountain bikes hidden behind some old, discarded pallets, the Courtneys saw Max walk to the parking lot to his car. Courtney let out a huge gasp, which startled Coco.

She asked, "What's wrong with you?"

Courtney answered, "You don't recognize it, do you? That's the same car that chased us the other day when we were headed to the police station. I'd know that car anywhere!"

Max got in his car and drove away. Of course, they couldn't follow him on their bikes, and Courtney asked.

"What do we do now?"

Coco looked at her and said, "Let's think! Where would he be going at 3:00 in the afternoon? Hmmm! There's always home, but probably not this early in the day. Maybe a girlfriend's house. I don't know!"

"Or maybe he's going to pick up his buddies and head over to their hideout!" Courtney said.

Coco responded, "You think so?" "I don't know, but I think it's the best idea we have right now."

"Yeah, let's go!" Coco said with excitement.

It was about a three-mile ride back to their grandmother's house. They finally got to the house and put their bikes in the garage. They began crossing the street to go into the woods when Nannie yelled out to them from the front porch.

"Where are you two 'hoodlums' going?"

She was going to walk to the ditch in the front lawn to pour something out from one of her cooking pans. You could tell she had been in the kitchen because she had her apron on. In fact, it was her favorite apron! Coco gave it to her on her fifty-fifth birthday. It said, "Grandkids do no wrong!" "Um, uh..." Both Courtneys were stammering, trying to think of what to say. Coco finally spoke. "Uh, hi, Nannie! We're gonna do some exploring in the woods." "Well, don't stay long; dinner will be ready in about thirty minutes, and to be honest, I don't know if I like you two going in the woods alone, anyway. Lanlad and I have been hearing about some crazy things going on lately." "Aw, Nannie, we'll be okay," Courtney replied. "Hang on!" Nannie said as she went back inside. After a few seconds, she came back out and had taken her apron off. Not only that, but she'd also even put her tennis shoes on.

She trotted over and said, "You don't mind if I do some exploring with you, do you?"

She really wasn't looking for an answer. It was just a polite way of saying, "I'm going with you two."

"I'd be worrying my head off if I let you go out in the woods by yourselves, so I'm going with you two."

The Courtneys mentioned that she might need to stay so dinner wouldn't get burned, but they were having spaghetti, and the meat needed to simmer for another twenty to thirty-five minutes, and she hadn't even started the noodles yet.

Well, the Courtneys didn't know what to do now. They went ahead and trekked into the woods but tried to steer away from the shack. Surprisingly, they had a better time than they thought they would have. They climbed trees, and even Nannie climbed a couple of smaller ones. Nannie came up with the great idea of having a scavenger hunt and gave them instructions.

"We'll all think of three items to find, and the first one to find them wins."

They had a tremendous amount of fun competing with each other. As they were looking for the different items, though, they had thoughtlessly gotten closer and closer to the shack. Nannie whispered to the girls to come back to her and let out a soft "shh." All three stood in a huddle, staring at the shack, which was about three-hundred feet away. They probably wouldn't have even noticed it, but the "rap" music coming from the shack had caught their attention. As the three of them were hidden behind some large bushes, they could hear voices whooping and hollering. The girls suspected it was the same teenagers they had already had dealings with. They strained very hard to see into the windows to see if they could see Max, but from three-hundred feet away and dirty windows, it was just too difficult to see much of anything. They looked to see if they could spot Max's car, too, but there was no way he could have driven to the shack unless there was a road they didn't know about. They were hoping for some kind of a hint that they were the same ones that were there before.

Then they heard one yell out, "Hey, I can't find the machete! It's missing."

Another one said something about the bowl being gone, too, and both Courtneys knew exactly what bowl he was talking about. Still, they didn't get any glimpse of anyone they had seen before when they were being chased earlier by them.

That was enough for Nannie!

She grabbed the girl's arms and quietly said, "Let's get back to the house!"

They kept their bodies down as low as they could, without crawling, and eventually returned to the house. Nannie told the girls to get cleaned up for supper. They finished washing their hands, and as they were coming down the stairs, they heard Nannie talking to Lanlad about their experience in the woods. He thought it was probably just a few teens goofing off but told Nannie that he would let the police know anyway about the shack and the boys. Lanlad dialed the police, and Desk Sergeant Harmon answered. Lanlad proceeded to tell him the information, and Sergeant Harmon reassured him he'd get someone to check on it but said it was probably nothing to be concerned with. Most likely a bunch of kids just hanging out. Lanlad told the Sergeant that was what he thought, as well. He thanked him, and they both hung up.

"I think I'll call Gordon and mention this to him, too," Lanlad told Nannie.

"That's a good idea!" Nannie replied.

Sergeant Harmon called Police Chief Moses and told him about his conversation with Lanlad. Chief Moses then called Gordon McLarin, the county's new game warden. Gordon was 29 years old, 6' 2", and beginning to gray around the sides of his hairline. He had started his career in north Alabama around Gadsden and was there for about three years. He'd only been in this county for six months, and it hadn't been the best of situations, and it sure wasn't the most pleasant county he'd ever served in. In that short time, he'd been shot at four times, ran off a dirt road by a speeding group of night hunters, and had to get an unlisted number because he'd received six or seven threatening calls at his house. Moses told him he was following up on a call from Hugh Hargis, who lived near the golf course. Gordon couldn't stop Moses long enough to tell him he'd just gotten off the phone with Mr. Hargis. Moses asked him if he'd seen any run-down shacks during any of his rounds in the woods.

"Well, just so happens that I did notice an old cabin the other day. I was off duty and doing a little hunting on Mr. Jasper's land. You know, he owns some land in that same area, near the golf course?"

"Of course, I know where you're talking about, Gordon. Don't forget, I've lived here all my life. You're the new kid on the block."

Gordon wasn't quite sure how to take the remark about being the new kid. When he last served as a game warden, the law enforcement folks helped one another and tried to be extra helpful. He had to always dig and scratch for anything he needed around this county.

"What about any kids? You know, like teenagers? Seen any of them?"

"No. The only teenagers I've seen have been with their dads hunting or ones old enough to hunt by themselves."

"You did go inside the shack, didn't cha?"

"Of course I did," Gordon replied, a little frustrated with the Sergeant. Moses seemed to be insinuating that Gordon was incompetent and incapable of doing his job. Gordon just tried to ignore it and continued.

Then Moses asked him, "Did you find anything strange or out of the ordinary?"

"Now that you mention it, Sergeant, there was something peculiar."

"Yeah, what was that?"

At this point in their conversation, Gordon was getting a strange feeling and didn't feel real comfortable telling Police Chief Moses about the machete and bowl of blood he'd found. He had to think quickly.

"So, what was so strange?" Police Chief Moses seemed a little too curious.

"Uh, it really wasn't that big of a deal. I just wasn't expecting it to look as 'straightened up' as it was."

"What do you mean?"

"Well, you could tell there had been people in it, and pretty recent. As if there had been some meeting."

"What gave you that idea?"

"Well, first of all, there were fresh ashes in the fireplace."

Moses interrupted, noticeably bothered.

"Ashes? In the summertime?"

"Yeah, I figured someone had cooked some hotdogs because I found a hotdog bun bag in the corner with some sticks. I think they used them to put the hotdogs on. There was also a broken bottle of liquor on the floor. It appeared to have been broken recently because the floor was still wet. Another thing was there were a couple of chairs, and they were placed near the table as if there had been a meeting."

"Sounds like you're just reaching for something now, boy."

Gordon didn't like Moses calling him boy. He felt as if Moses was doing what he could to belittle and demean him. Gordon wanted to respond with his disgust but bit his tongue.

"I bet that it's just some hunters that use that cabin as a little resting place while they're hunting."

Chief Moses replied, "Well, that's what I was thinking the whole time anyway. Gotta go. Gotta another phone call. If you notice anything else suspicious, let me know."

"Suspicious? You're the one acting so suspiciously." Almost as if he was trying to hide something, Gordon thought to himself as he placed the receiver back into its cradle. "I need to do some investigating myself and better keep it to myself!" he thought.

"Yeah, what!" the person on the other end of the phone answered gruffly. Timidly, the caller replied.

"All I know is this new game warden could be trouble. He seems the type to go snooping where he doesn't belong."

"Nobody asked your opinion. You just make sure I get any information that you think will be important. And don't call me from the station anymore; it makes me nervous!"

CHAPTER THREE: THE COURTNEYS MEET GORDON MCLARIN, THE GAME WARDEN

"Yum, yum! Spaghetti! I love spaghetti!" said Lanlad. Spaghetti was his favorite supper. It was both the Courtneys' favorite meal, too, well, besides pizza. The dinner conversation was a little more exciting than usual. They recounted all the fun details that they had had in the woods, the scavenger hunt, and watching Nannie climb some trees with them, but it gradually got more somber when the conversation turned to the shack and the teenagers they'd seen. And just as the Courtneys expected, her grandparents told them they weren't allowed to go into the woods alone anymore. The Courtneys were very disappointed at that decision, but they understood. It was always best to ere on the side of precaution.

They finished their spaghetti and went outside and threw the frisbee around. Lanlad came outside and asked them if they wanted to drive the riding lawnmower, which he let them do while he was there to watch. They jumped at the opportunity and had a great time riding all over their huge yard. It was getting dark, so they put up the lawnmower and, went inside, and took a shower. They put their pajamas on and came downstairs to watch some television with Nannie and Lanlad. Lanlad asked Nannie if it would be okay if he and the girls had some popcorn. She accommodated them and even made some caramel popcorn to munch on. One of Lanlad's favorite snacks. They all had another great evening together and then went to their bedrooms to sleep. This time, the Courtneys didn't forget to get their lists out and pray.

Gordon wasn't normally the curious type, but things had gotten a little weird, and he couldn't help himself from looking into it all the questions he had. A few days had gone by, and nothing out of the ordinary had happened. That is, nothing anyone made a big deal about. There were a couple of break-ins in the Colonial Heights Subdivision, one in the Hillwood area, and a couple of nights ago, Barton's grocery store was broken into. Now, there was a strange incident! There was no apparent evidence of anyone actually breaking in, no door jambs pried open, and no windows broken. The only evidence was the safe that had been cracked open and the day's earnings had been taken. The strangest thing, though, was about twenty-five frozen chickens had been stolen. He couldn't imagine why someone would take one frozen chicken, much less twenty-five. He put off thinking about the questions because he had to go to work.

Gordon's nightly routine was usually the same. He was always on the outlook for night hunters. Occasionally, he would catch two or three a month. He would take his mechanical deer, whom he'd named Bambi, and place it into an open field. Its head and tail could be moved by remote control, which made Bambi an even better decoy. Gordon would then hide in his truck and sit and wait. Night hunters were notorious for going out and looking for deer. Some would try and find that one-in-a-million buck with the biggest rack recorded in hunting history, while others just wanted to put more meat in the freezer. And they knew if they could find some in the fields, it would make for easy killing. All they had to do was shine their headlights into their eyes, and the deer would freeze, and then kaboom! Poor Bambi had numerous scars where it had been hit so many times by night hunters who had been fooled by the decoy. This particular night was very cloudy and dark. Gordon was on patrol nearing the neighborhood of the old shack. As he peered through the woods, he thought he saw some glimmers of light. He got out of his truck and started toward it. When he got about two-hundred feet, he saw the flickers of lights immediately go out. At seventy-five feet, he thought he heard some talking. Actually, whispering. When he stepped onto the porch to announce to those inside who he was, the front door opened slightly, and a black cat ran out with a terrifying screech. It startled and caught Gordon off guard so much that he dropped his flashlight and broke the bulb. That's when he heard what sounded like eight to ten people scrambling inside to get out. Some had jumped out of the windows; others braved going right out of the front door.

It was so dark Gordon didn't see them coming and was knocked down. He was quick enough to grab one by the pant leg, but the culprit shook loose and was able to kick Gordon in the mouth. Gordon got up and took his .357 Smith and Wesson out of its holster. He shot up into the air, hoping that they would stop. They knew he wouldn't shoot at them, so they just kept running. It was too dark to try and run after them, so he decided to go inside and see what he could find. As soon as he stepped inside, he was reminded of the horrible smell from his first encounter at this shack. He rubbed his sore jaw and found that he had a little trickle of blood where he'd gotten kicked. After using his shirt sleeve to wipe it off, he felt around the room to see if he could find any evidence of some wrongdoings and walked right into a chair. First, his jaw gets kicked in, and now his shin gets bruised up. He held back the temptation to use some choice words. As he continued to feel around the room, he found some matches and a candle on the mantle above the fireplace. It didn't give him much light, but it gave him enough to keep from getting hit by anything else. He walked over to the table in the middle of the room and noticed that it was covered with a thick red liquid. "Ugh, blood again!" he thought.

He also saw what looked like animal hair...black animal hair. The front door opened, and Gordon quickly drew his service revolver, but it was only the black cat again. The one that made him break his flashlight. He picked it up and started petting it, and before he realized it, he had blood all over his hands and shirt. He instantly dropped the cat. Where was this coming from? As he looked closer, he saw that the cat didn't have a tail. It had recently been cut off. "I guess they were playing animal surgeon," he said out loud to himself. Was this some cult or just a bunch of kids having what they might call a good time? He needed to talk to someone about this, but who could he trust?

The next day, both girls had an opportunity to make another run to Ice Cream Charlie's. He gave the girls their favorite bowl of chocolate fudge brownie with extra chocolate syrup, and they started digging in. It hadn't been five minutes and Coco let out a huge laugh and was pointing at Courtney at the same time. Courtney said, "What?"

Coco was laughing to talk, so she just pointed at Courtney's shirt. Courtney looked down, and she saw there was ice cream and chocolate fudge sauce all over the front of her tee shirt. It was a direct hit to both their funny bones. They busted into a chorus of laughter. Coco had to bend over to get another breath because she was laughing so hard. When she did, her chair shot out from under her into the man's shin sitting at the table next to them. Of course, then their laughter graduated to an outburst! She immediately got up and picked up the chair, then turned to the man and apologized. Gordon forced a grin while rubbing his already sore shin and said, "That's alright! It must have been a funny joke you just heard."

Extremely embarrassed, Coco said, "Uh, um, yes, sir." Charlie glanced over at their table and gave a stern look well, as stern as Charlie could give.

Courtney grabbed Coco by the arm and said, "I can't believe you hit a cop."

"What?"

"Look, he has a gun."

Coco glanced over at the man, and there it was, big as light! They broke into another string of laughter, but this time quieter and more subdued. While the Courtneys were enjoying themselves, they didn't notice the group of teenage boys coming through Ice Cream Charlie's door. They had walked up to the ice cream counter, and one of the boys made a smart remark.

"Give me some of that Rocky Road ice cream."

Then he began singing the tune to the "Rocky" movies while trying to imitate Rocky's boxing moves when Rocky was climbing up the city hall steps in the first movie of the series. The other boys roared in laughter, calling him stupid and pushing each other around. Charlie was about to tell the boys to quiet down when Max walked in. He told the boys to shut up and order or get out. They instantly calmed down but gave Max looks that could have killed him.

Charlie said, "Thanks, Max, and how's business at the convenience store?"

"Oh, it's okay, Charlie. They're working me to death."

Right behind Max walked in Robby Barton, son of the owner of Barton's grocery. Charlie greeted him, as well, and Robby nodded back.

"Sorry to hear about your dad's store getting robbed. Tell your dad to give me a call." Robby responded with fake interest, "Huh? Oh, yeah! Me, too, and I sure will."

All the commotion had caught everyone's attention and, especially Gordon's. Coco looked to say something and noticed Courtney was holding a menu up, covering her face. Coco asked her, "What are you doing?"

"That's him. That's the guy who recognized me from the shack."

Immediately, Coco picked up a menu and did the same.

"What are we going to do?" Courtney asked.

Coco just shook her head from side to side and pantomimed, "I don't know." Courtney had just pulled her menu down to take a quick peek. Bad move! Robby was looking around the parlor and about to sit down when his eyes and Courtney's eyes met at the exact same time. His hind end hadn't even touched his chair before he got up and walked over to their table.

"Well, well, well! Long time, no see, girls. How have you two been doing? Ran into anyone we know lately."

Robby gave an evil laugh and leaned in hard looking directly at each one of them, and said, "I'm sure we'll be seeing you real soon."

Max called for Robby to come over to him. Regretfully, he left the girl's table to see what Max wanted. Max told him to sit down and then said, "Don't make a scene. We have to be careful. We can't give anybody cause to have any suspicions about us."

Gordon had been watching the whole ordeal with much curiosity. He wasn't sure if these boys were just playing games, or if they were going to be some real problems. He finished his ice cream and got up to pay his bill. As he passed the girls' table, he asked them, "Are you two in any trouble?"

The Courtneys looked at each other, not really knowing how to answer the man's question. He gave them his business card and said, "If you are and need someone to talk to, just call me. I'm the new game warden for the county, and my name is Gordon McLarin."

He paid his bill and told Charlie thanks and goodbye. He walked to the boys' table and said, "You boys be sure to stay outta trouble, you hear?" He snickered within himself for using Police Chief Moses' southern twang.

The Courtneys sat completely frozen, not saying a word. This was totally uncharacteristic of them. Hardly ever could you find them when they weren't making some kind of noise, that is, unless they were sleeping.

Max snapped his fingers to get the boys' attention and said, "Let's go over to their table and, hey, be sure to make it look like we know them. Remember, we don't want to raise any suspicions."

The boys slowly got up and slowly walked to the girl's table. They pulled some chairs up, surrounding them like a bunch of Apache Indians surrounding a wagon train. Max said, "So we finally have a chance to get a good look at the two of you. You two sure have caused us some grief."

"Yeah, look!" One of them rolled up his sleeve and showed a battle scar from getting knocked into the fifty-gallon drums.

"Now, Billy, be nice. I'm sure these nice girls didn't mean any harm. We've got just a few questions that we want to ask you. You got some time for us?"

Coco was never one to diddle-daddle in a tough situation. Sometimes, she made some bad decisions in her hastiness, but this time, it didn't matter, and she hoped Courtney would follow her lead. She looked straight into Max's eyes and said, "The only time I have for you is this time!"

At that moment, she threw the rest of her ice cream into Max's face and jumped up to head for the door. It caught them all by such surprise that it gave Courtney time to do the same with the remainder of her ice cream. She threw the bowl straight up in the air, and as fate would have it, it landed right on Robby's new Adidas tennis shoes. As they were trying to slip through the circle, one of the boys was able to grab Coco by the arm, and another tripped Courtney and picked her up after she fell. They both thought their proverbial gooses were cooked.

Charlie was busy back in the back of his shop, and there really hadn't been enough commotion to get his attention. At that same time, though, Gordon stepped back in and said, "I need to see you two girls, please. Are these your bikes out here? I might have accidentally bumped into one of them as I was leaving."

He'd been watching the episode from his truck the whole time. Immediately, the boys unhanded each girl and acted like they were all friends and just playing around. The Courtneys paid Charlie and walked out the front door, happy to be alive and very thankful to this game warden.

Max was wiping off the fudge brownie from his face and said as they were leaving, "See you, girls! See you real soon!" Robby was headed to the restroom to wash off his unfortunate mess. His mom and dad would kill him if they saw his new shoes like this. He was steaming. He hadn't been this mad since his biology teacher wouldn't give him one point to change an F to a D. If the teacher had done it, Robby wouldn't have had to go to summer school two summers ago. But he got even with him. He found out where the teacher lived and set his backyard storage building on fire a couple of weeks later. It burned everything in it, even his riding lawnmower. Only Max and a couple of others knew he was the culprit of that little stunt.

When the girls got outside, they found that their bikes were perfectly sound. They looked at the man, and Coco said, "Hey, what gives? Our bikes are fine. I thought you said you'd hit one of them."

"Don't be afraid and just act like something really did happen to one of your bikes. Trust me, please." The Courtneys didn't make it a habit to talk to strangers, but this time, they compromised a little on their philosophy. They would listen but still not talk. They could have won an Oscar for their stellar performance. The boys inside Ice Cream Charlie's watched intently to see what transpired between this game warden and the two girls, whom they still didn't know by name. The Oscar performance was good enough to fool the boys, and they eventually went back to their business, except for Max and Robby. Their steely eyes remained on both Courtneys and Gordon.

Gordon appreciated the girls following his lead and asked one more request, "Do me a favor and get on your bikes. Ride to Walmart, and I'll meet you there in fifteen minutes. I'll stay here and make sure your friends don't follow you."

The Courtneys, still unsure about what was taking place, still hadn't said a word to Gordon. They got on their bikes and took off in the direction of Wal-Mart. One of the boys said, "Let's go after them, Max!"

"Just cool your jets! We'll have another chance to get our hands on those two little menaces. I'll make sure of that."

CHAPTER FOUR: CHURCH AND MORE ICE CREAM

Gordon stayed outside as if he was doing other business to make sure the boys didn't go after the girls. He really needed to talk to the Courtneys but wasn't sure if they would go to Wal-Mart and wait for him. He whispered a prayer that they would. The Courtneys took turns praying out loud that the Lord would give them wisdom on how to handle this situation. After they prayed, they agreed on a plan. They would go to Wal-Mart and go inside where the arcade games were. There were always a lot of people, mostly kids their age, playing the games. They felt they would be safe enough there. Mr. Thompson would also be there. He was the greeter at the Wal-Mart front door. He had been retired for ten years.

He loved seeing and meeting people, and that's why he applied for that particular job. Coco knew him because he and his wife went to her grandparent's church. He was one of the church greeters there, too. As soon as they got there, they said hello and asked him if he knew the new game warden. He said, "Oh, sure. That would be Gordon McLarin. Seems like a wonde... Hi, do you need a cart today?" He interrupted himself three different times like that before he finished answering the question.

"Now, where was I? Oh, yeah. Gordon seems like a wonderful fellow. He's even been visiting our church. You won't find him there on some Sunday mornings, though, because he spends the whole night before looking for night hunters. Why do you ask?"

Before they could answer, Mr. Thompson turned around and asked another customer if he could stick a red sticker on the item she was bringing back. He had to do that with returned items. At the same time,

Gordon walked in and asked the Courtneys if they wouldn't mind sitting down with him in the snack bar. They felt a little safer since they had talked to Mr. Thompson and agreed to his request.

Mr. Thompson looked around and saw the Courtneys and Gordon walking toward the snack room and called Gordon, "Hey, Gordon, you be careful. Those two were asking a lot of questions about you. They might be up to something."

He chuckled, and Gordon said, "Thanks for the advice, Mr. Thompson. I'll be careful. They do look a little dangerous."

Before sitting down, they brushed off the food remains that an earlier customer had left behind on the table.

"Well, let me get started. First of all, I appreciate you two trusting me and doing as I asked. I know it's not a very smart thing to do these days with all the strange characters running loose. I'm glad you checked up on me with Mr. Thompson. Maybe that will give me a little more credibility with you."

Coco was the first one to break their code of silence. "It did help a little, but I don't mind telling you, we both are very curious why you helped and what you would want to talk to us about."

"And by the way," Courtney interjected, thanks for the help over at Ice Cream Charlie's."

"Sure, that's okay! What was that about anyway?"

They looked at each other and didn't know if they should entrust him with the recent events or not. After a time of silence, Gordon opened up and said, "You don't have to tell me anything you don't want to, but I've been experiencing some strange things lately and thought you two might be able to give me some insight. I wouldn't have thought anything until I saw what happened at Charlie's. Bear with me while I explain. I've only been to this county for a couple of months, and they haven't been the most pleasant months of my life, I must say. There are a lot of good folks that live here, but this county has more than its fair share of 'difficult' folks. Since I am in law enforcement, I'm in contact with many sheriffs, policemen, and other authorities. Just about every time I've needed help on a particular unlawful situation here, it seemed as if no one wanted to give me any assistance. Hey, how about a soft drink or something?"

Their mouths were a little dry, so they agreed. Gordon got up and went through the concession line. He came back with a Coke for each one of them, plus some sugar cookies and chocolate chip cookies. They both licked their lips when they saw the cookies.

"Oh, I love Otis Spunkmeyer cookies!" Coco expressed.

"They're the best!"The Courtneys agreed. They ate their snack and continued listening very patiently as Gordon spoke again.

"Well, back to those recent instances I was referring to. Most of the time spent on my job as a game warden, is mostly in the woods. I check for hunting licenses, watch out for night hunters, and basically just make sure people are within the law when they are in the woods. The other day, I came across something very curious."

Gordon told them of the time he was in the shack for the first time and what he had found there. He couldn't help but notice the look of shock on both of their faces. He asked, "What? Did I say something wrong?"

Coco answered him without thinking, "I think we were there at the same time."

"Yeah, inside the shack," Courtney added.

"What? You mean you two were in that old run-down cabin at the same time I was? Why didn't you say anything?"

Courtney jumped back into the conversation and said, "Cause we were scared to death! That's why."

Coco added, "We didn't know if you were one of those crazy teenage boys that were in there earlier and coming back for something."

This caught Gordon's attention, "What's that? Are you referring to those teenagers at Charlie's? They were in the shack before I was. Where were you because I sure didn't see you?"

Courtney continued. "Remember that old piece of plywood that was standing up against the wall?"

"You two were behind there?"

Gordon was excited! He finally felt like he was beginning to make heads and tails of all this confusion.

"So, you're telling me you two were in the shack before me or the boys, right?"

Both girls replied, "Yessir."

"What were you two doing out there?"

"Well, we've always loved hiking and exploring around in the woods until just recently. My grandparents told us we couldn't go out there alone anymore."

Gordon asked, "Why'd they tell you that?"

They told him of the time when they and Nannie went into the woods and how it disturbed her so much that she told Lanlad, and he immediately told the Police Chief about it. Gordon slipped off his hat and scratched his head.

"So, that's why Moses called me that day."

"Huh?" both Courtneys said in unison. Gordon went on to explain about the call from Police Chief Moses and all three continued comparing notes for another forty-five more minutes.

"You girls have been a tremendous help. Thank you very much." Both Courtneys began to shoot him a barrage of questions like what he planned on doing now. What he thought those boys were doing out there in the woods? Did he think the boys were the ones committing all the robberies? Was there something they could do to help? What was he…?

Gordon held his hands up, interrupting them. "Whoa! Hold on a minute! First of all, you two need to stay out of trouble and not get involved. This could be more dangerous than meets the eye!"

"Yeah, but," Coco exclaimed.

"No buts about it. You two have been more helpful than you could imagine already. Now it's time to let me manage the rest of it. I'll tell you what, if you hear of anything that you think could help me, then be sure to call me. That would be a tremendous help."

Disappointedly Courtney asked, "Come on, Mr. McLarin. Isn't there something we could help with?"

"I'm sorry, girls, but as I said, there could be a whole lot more to this, and if anything happened to you two because of it, I'd feel terrible, to say the least. I gotta go, and you girls better get going before it gets dark. See you around. Maybe I'll see you at church tonight."

In all the excitement, the Courtneys had forgotten that it was Wednesday and they had church. They jumped on their mountain bikes and took off for Coco's grandparent's house. Their church had a mid-week prayer meeting that the adults attended while the children had Bible study classes. The church would also have supper at 5:30 for only $2.50 per person. What a deal! Lori Lemon, who the kids nicknamed 'Lemondrop' was their teacher. She was 27 years old, 5' 10", with long, thick blonde hair and a sleek, athletic build. All the kids loved her. She was extremely creative and so much fun. She would create many interesting ways to learn about the Bible. The students especially loved to play a game that Lori had made up called Jitters. Each child would be given a number and would have to gather really close around Lori. Then, she would throw a nerf ball up in the air while the kids walked slowly away. She would then yell out one of their numbers.

Whoever had that number would have to run back and grab the ball and then yell 'jitters'. That meant wherever the other students were had to freeze in place. The person who retrieved the ball would have a chance to answer a question about what they had been studying that night, and if they got it right, they would have the chance to throw the ball at someone. Points were scored by answering the Bible questions and for hitting someone with the ball. It was Courtney's favorite game, and they learned a lot about the Bible when playing it. The evening had gone by all too fast, in fact, they didn't even get to finish their game. When Nannie and Lanlad walked in to get the girls and someone was throwing a ball at the same time. It missed the intended victim and was headed directly for Nannie's head. All the kids and Lori froze. Lanlad caught it about five inches from impact! Lori came running over and apologized. Nannie told her it was all right, that there wasn't any harm done. Then Lanlad said, "Does this mean I get a free throw?"

At first, the statement caught Lori by surprise, but then she realized that Lanlad was going to have a little fun. "Oh, yes, sir! That's the rule! You can try and hit any one of them!" When the kids heard what Lori said to

Lanlad, they started running all over the activity room, trying to dodge any potential Lanlad missiles.

That's when Gordon walked in to help. Nannie and Lanlad waved and said hi as if they knew him quite well. He grabbed a couple of boys and told Lanlad to take his best shot. "Here, Mr. Hargis! I've got a couple of 'em you can hit." Coco wasn't surprised to see Gordon, but she was surprised to find out that her grandparents and Gordon knew each other.

Most of the children had been picked up by their parents within a few minutes, but some were still throwing the ball around or playing tag. Courtney and Coco were fighting with foam rubber noodles. One would hit the other and then run away and the other one would repeat the same process as soon as one reached the other. They looked like they were fencing at one time when they got tangled up and fell on each other. After falling down and having a big laugh, Coco nudged Courtney and said, "Look!"

She was pointing at Lori and Gordon, who were holding hands. What was this all about, they thought. Lanlad called for the Courtneys to get ready to leave and asked them if they'd like to go to Ice Cream Charlie's. He also asked Gordon and Lori if they were interested in going. They said yes, but Gordon mentioned he couldn't stay too long because he had to go on patrol to look for potential night hunters.

They all arrived at Ice Cream Charlie's within a few minutes of leaving the church.

"How are you folks doing tonight? What can I get you? I think I already know what these two want."

Charlie turned to get a couple of scoops of chocolate fudge brownie and mumbled, "Twice in one day, huh?" Both girls stealthily put their forefinger across their lips and shushed Charlie. He smiled. When everyone finally got seated, the conversation was light and fun. Eventually, it turned to the current events of the last couple of weeks. Lori started and said to Gordon, "What do you make of all the stuff that's been happening lately, Gordon?"

Up to this point, Gordon hadn't said very much to anyone about what he knew. Not even Lori. Gordon answered her and said, "Don't know much about the robberies but I found a couple of mysterious things in that run-down shack."

"Like what?" Lori asked.

"I figured on finding beer cans, maybe food, and typical stuff like that, but what I didn't figure on finding was a bowl of blood, a machete, and a cat with a chopped-off tail." He proceeded to tell them about his episode the night he scared off that bunch of teens from the cabin.

"What was really strange, though, was the way Police Chief Moses corresponds with me when I bring to his attention some of these issues. He's been quite evasive and vague with his responses. Won't give me any details about anything and won't answer any of my questions. Although, he acts overly curious about how much I know and what my involvement is."

Nannie asked Gordon, "You think it's safe for kids to be playing by themselves out in the woods with all this mess going on?"

After looking at the Courtneys, Gordon answered, "Well, That's a tough one! I think it would have to depend on the kids and how sharp they are. Take these two, pointing at both Courtneys. They seem to be pretty sharp. I believe they could handle just about anything that came their way."

The Courtneys were really beginning to like Gordon. First, he saves them from, who knows what could have happened earlier today in Ice

Cream Charlie's, then he goes to the same church Coco's grandparents do, he and Lori like each other, and last but not least, this last statement he made about them was pretty nice. Nannie, seeing that mischievous look in their eyes, said, "That doesn't mean you two are allowed to go back out there without adult supervision, though."

"Aww, Nannie," Coco complained.

"You can aww, Nannie, all you want, but it won't make any difference to me."

"Sorry, girls. I have to agree with Nannie at this time since there seem to be such weird and strange happenings going on in the woods. Let me do some more investigating, and I'll let all of you know whatever I find out."

Lanlad agreed and then said, "Well, we better get going. It's getting late, and you don't want to see Nannie nodding off. It's a scary sight. Ain't it, girls?"

Nannie gave Lanlad one of those familiar looks that he'd seen so many times in their thirty-eight years of marriage. Gordon quickly spoke to get some of the heat off of Lanlad, "Thanks for inviting me and Lori tonight. We had a wonderful time. And you two must be terrific grandparents to allow these girls ice cream twice in one day."

"What?" Nannie exclaimed.

"Uh, oh!" Gordon knew he'd said the wrong thing, and just when they were getting to like this guy. As they were walking out the door, you could hear Nannie going on and on about ice cream's calories, fat grams, and sugar intake. Lanlad then whispered to the girls loud enough for Nannie to hear, "Why didn't you invite me today."

"And Lanlad, you're not a particularly good influence either," Nannie said sternly.

"Aw, Nannie. A little sugar is good for the body. Just look at mine."

Lanlad did love sweets. Especially ice cream. He had been known to eat a whole half gallon in one night before. Both girls turned around and mouthed to Gordon, "Thanks a lot!"

Gordon mouthed back with hands raised, "I'm sorry. I didn't know!"

Unnoticed, or at least he thought so, was a man in the corner talking on the phone. "Yeah, I'm sure! I was sitting only a couple of tables away. The game warden said he was going to continue looking into it and see what he could discover. I tell you. I think this guy is gonna be trouble!"

A voice on the other end of the phone interrupted, "Nobody asked you to think, did they? You leave the thinking to me, and just be sure to keep me informed of anything you find out or hear."

"Yessir!"

"Why haven't you started the car yet, Gordon?" Lori asked in Gordon's parked car.

"Shh, there he is," And with that, Gordon grabbed Lori close to him and kissed her passionately. He continued to do so until the man, who had been on the phone, got into his truck and drove away.

"Wow, Gordon! What was that all about?"

"Oh, I'm sorry. I had to make sure the man inside didn't see me watching him, and that was the best way I could think of at the moment."

"You mean, you were just acting?"

"Well, not really, but..."

"But what?"

"Let me explain, Lori."

"Go right ahead. I can't wait to hear this one."

"Well, inside, while we were eating and talking, I happened to notice a fellow sitting a couple of tables from us in the corner. Every now and then, I would catch him taking a look at us, and it appeared he was overly interested in what we were talking about. When we got up to pay, he pulled out his cell phone and started talking to someone."

Lori said, "Are you sure you're not a little paranoid, maybe?"

"I don't think so, Lori. I got his tag, and I'll run it by the police dispatcher to see if I can find anything."

Then, with a sly-looking smile, Lori said, "Well, I'll let you off the hook this time, but the next you grab me like that and kiss me, you better be thinking about me and only me. Got it?"

"Yes, ma'am!"

Gordon took Lori home, walked her to her front door, and told her he'd talk to her tomorrow. He was about to kiss her good night when she pulled away really quick and said, "Let that be a lesson to you to keep you from forgetting what I told earlier you," with a devilish grin, she grabbed his chin and gave him a goodnight kiss.

He got in his car and drove home to his small, lonely apartment. While he was in his driveway, he called the police dispatcher and asked her to run a license plate for him. He gave her the man's tag number, and within a matter of seconds, the dispatcher said, "I'm showing that tag belongs to the owner, Mike Shealy. In fact, he's a patrolman here on the force."

To cover any suspicion, Gordon quickly faked a response, "Oh, Yeah, oh, yeah. Good ole Mike!"

Hopefully, the dispatcher didn't think anything about it. As he was getting out of his truck, a rock came flying through the passenger's side window. Luckily, the shattered glass didn't hit him. He jumped out of his vehicle, took out his revolver, and stood still. He then heard a bunch of guys saying, "Hurry up. Get into the car. Let's go!"

He saw a car speeding away but couldn't identify it. With tires squealing, Gordon backed out of his driveway. When he looked down the street, the car was almost out of sight. Gordon was able to see that it made a right turn. He stepped on the accelerator to chase after it, and his truck started sputtering. It was out of gas! Whoever he was chasing must have siphoned it out because he had just filled it up the day before. After slapping the steering wheel, he located the rock that they had thrown and found a note tied to it.

It read, "Keep your nose out where it doesn't belong, or you just might get hurt or maybe worse! You're way out of your league!" Whoever thought this idea would scare Gordon away from his investigation didn't know him very well. All it did was make him that much more determined to get some answers.

CHAPTER FIVE: JASPER'S SHOOTING HOUSE

"Boy, am I tired!" Courtney said with droopy eyes.

Coco asked, "I wonder why no one ever says, 'girl' instead of a 'boy'?"

"What are you talking about?" Courtney inquired.

"Well, you just started your statement with the 'boy.' Why don't you start using 'girl'?"

Courtney rolled her eyes and replied, "If it will make you shut up, I will. Now, 'girl,' go to sleep."

Coco said, "Can't, yet."

"Why not? I'm tired!" Courtney answered.

"You forgot this time."

"Forgot what?"

"We gotta pray, remember?"

Courtney retorted, "I wouldn't have forgotten. You just didn't give me enough time to remember!"

"Oh, good one, Court." They both got their lists out and prayed through them and finally got to sleep at about 12:30 that morning.

A couple of hours later, Courtney woke Coco up.

"What? What? Courtney answered with frustration. I was having the best dream ever."

"Didn't you hear that? Hear what?"

"I thought I heard some noise downstairs."

"Are you crazy? You must have been dreaming."

The noise they heard next was convincing enough for both of them. They got up, put their robes and house shoes on, and quietly crept downstairs. They thought it might be Nannie. Many times, she would be up late working on some kind of church project or putting something into the crockpot for the next day's lunch or supper. The Courtneys were holding each other so tightly as they walked down the stairs that they looked like Siamese twins. When they turned the corner into the kitchen, four boys grabbed them, covered the girls' mouths, hauled them outside, and slapped blindfolds over their eyes.

One time during the abduction, Lanlad thought he'd heard something but decided it was nothing. The boys dragged the girls into the woods, with both of them kicking and screaming. Of course, their screams were muffled by the boy's hands over their mouths. They were petrified! They both had a fairly good hunch about where they were going. The shack! The boys said nothing the whole way. Up one step, then the next, onto the porch, and through the front door.

Earlier, when the noise startled Lanlad, he attempted to get back to sleep but he couldn't and decided to get up and get a drink of water. On the way down, he glanced into the room where the Courtneys slept and thought it odd they weren't in their beds. Maybe they were downstairs, he thought. He walked down and looked around but couldn't find them anywhere. Now he was worried! He called for Nannie to hurry and come down. She raced down and asked what was wrong.

"The girls are gone!"

"What? Where would they have gone this hour of the night?"

"I can't imagine. Look!"

The kitchen door was ajar, and on the deck was one of Coco's house shoes. In the scuffle with the boys, one fell off onto the back deck. They both ran outside and called for them, but there was no answer.

"Oh, Lanlad, I'm scared. What are we going to do?" as she leaned into Lanlad's arms.

After they got into the shack, Robbie took off the blindfolds. That's when the Courtneys realized they were in a different shack. As they duct-taped each of their wrists and ankles to the chairs they were seated in, the Courtneys began to look around. It was very eerie, to say the least! This was a place much smaller with lit candles all placed in various areas on the floor, windowsills, vacant chairs, and tables. There were about nine or ten boys inside. The same ones who chased them in the alley and tried to harass them at Ice Cream Charlie's. It would seem that Max's threat of seeing them again finally came true. Max started the interrogation.

"First of all, I'd like to thank you, girls, for making it so easy for my compadres here to seize and bring you to our little abode. You two have been making it a habit of disturbing a couple of our plans lately."

As Max took his ballcap and placed it back on backward, he said, "What are we going to do with you two? You have become real pests. But, first, some answers to a few questions like, what you two were doing in the shack earlier this week?"

Neither did Courtney know what to say.

"It would be very wise for you two to speak up. My patience is wearing thin! You both have been a real pain in the neck."

Not surprisingly, Coco spoke first. "Um, um, we were just goofing off and found the shack and wanted to look inside it. That's when you guys came in, and we hid behind a piece of plywood."

"That's where I saw this little minion," Robby said as he pushed Courtney in the head.

"Leave me alone!" Courtney yelled, struggling to get out of the chair.

"Ooh, she a tough one!" one of the boys remarked. Max told him to shut up and asked the girls another set of questions.

"What did you hear while you were in there?"

"Nothing worth hearing." Courtney snorted.

"You are a feisty one, but don't push it, little girl. A couple of these boys would love to bash your head in!"

"Look," Coco said, "We didn't mean to be any trouble. Just let us go, and we promise we'll not say a word."

"Yeah, and we all believe in the Easter Bunny!"

All the boys got a kick out of that remark and let out a couple of chuckles.

Lanlad thought about calling Chief Moses, but he didn't want to get him involved since he heard what Gordon had said about his peculiar behavior of late, so he called Gordon instead. He told him that the girls were gone and didn't know what to do. Gordon had just gotten in from his evening patrol and told Lanlad that he'd come right over. It didn't take him but ten minutes to get to the Hargis' house. They were visibly shaken. They all went into the kitchen and sat down. They didn't want to think it, but was it possible that they could have been kidnapped?

"I am going to go to that old shack and see if anything is happening there."

"Mind if I tag along?"

"Well, I don't know, Mr. Hargis," Lanlad interrupted.

"Look, Gordon. It's my granddaughter and her best friend. I can't just sit here. Let me help."

"Okay. I probably could use the help. Let's go."

"Y'all, please be careful," Nannie begged.

One of the boys hollered out, "I say we quit wasting our time and slap them around a little."

Others chimed in and agreed openly.

"Shut up! Max yelled again. I gotta think." He got as close to the girl's faces as he could and asked, "What does this game warden have to do with any of this stuff? Is he checking us out?"

"Yeah, he's been trailing you and will soon get some evidence to put you all in jail." Courtney smarted off.

"Yeah, yeah, right. Talking about evidence, what did he do with our machete and that bowl of blood?"

Coco answered, "We don't know!"

Gordon and Lanlad were about seventy-five feet from the shack. They saw a little light inside but couldn't see anything of substance.

"What do you think we should do?" Lanlad asked.

Gordon answered, "You stay here. I'll sneak up to the door and rush in and take them by surprise."

"And what are you gonna do if there's more of them than you can manage?"

"Yeah, good point. I know. I'll shoot a couple of shots in the air and tell them to come out."

"You think it'll work?"

"You got a better idea?"

Lanlad shook his head.

"Okay, here goes!"

Bam! Bam! Bam! Bam!

"Hey, You boys in there. Come out of there, right now!"

Out came running six or seven men. Immediately, Lanlad and Gordon realized they'd made a mistake. They were just some hunters who were using the shack as a place to rest before they went hunting later that morning.

After Max had made the remark about not believing in the Easter bunny, a couple of the boys shoved each other and started to wrestle back and forth. One of the boys got out of balance and accidentally knocked over one of the kerosene lamps. The kerosene splashed in the direction of one of the candles on the floor and burst into flames. Within minutes, the fire had swiftly traveled to the other candles and some old drapes hanging from one of the windows increasing the fire's intensity. The Courtneys started screaming and struggling to untie themselves but to no avail. The boys ran out as quickly as they could.

They jumped into their various vehicles and hurried away. Robby Barton was already in his truck. He saw the flames quickly consuming the old shack. He jumped out of his truck and ran back inside to try and free the Courtneys.

Frustrated, he said, "I don't know why I'm doing this. Maybe it's because I have a sister your age!"

Both girls and Robby were continuously coughing because the smoke had gotten unbearable. All of Robby's life, he had suffered from a chronic case of asthma, and his breathing was becoming more and more shallow and labored with each breath. Battling to untie the girls from the chairs, he struggled just as much to get enough oxygen to his lungs. After a few seconds, he passed out without any success in untying them. The Courtneys were hacking and choking too much to yell any longer for help. They couldn't help but wonder if this was how they would die. If you could have heard inside the girl's heads, you would have heard both of them silently calling out for the Lord's protection. As the fire intensified, the smoke filled the whole room. The Courtneys were overcome by the smoke and passed out.

"Sorry, guys! We thought you were someone else." Gordon apologized.

"Hey, look!" One of the hunters was pointing in the direction of a fire, which must have been about a quarter of a mile away.

Another hunter said, "That looks like it might be Mr. Jasper's old shooting house. When Mr. Jasper was younger and hunted quite a bit, he'd built him a very small cabin where he'd sit on his front porch behind some camouflaged wall and wait for the deer to come to him.

"Come on, let's get over there," Gordon yelled. By the time they got there, the house was completely engulfed in flames. There was nothing anyone could do but watch it burn down to the ground. The local fire volunteers did what they could to make sure there weren't any remnants of any embers that could cause any further damage. Gordon apologized to the hunters once again for the misunderstanding. He thought about checking to see if their hunting licenses were up to date or if they had any at all, but there were more pressing issues he needed to handle. They all walked back to the little shack.

Lanlad and Gordon went back to the Hargis' home, hopeless since they still didn't have any knowledge of what had happened to the girls.

When they walked to the front door, Gordon asked, "What are you doing here?"

It was patrolman Mike Shealy. The man he had seen using the phone earlier in the corner at Ice Cream Charlie's. He was sitting down on the front steps of the Hargis' house, and he had a good-sized bandage on his left arm. Lanlad went inside and shouted for Nannie. After coming downstairs, she immediately gave him a big hug and then proceeded to tell him what she'd discovered since he and Gordon had left earlier that morning.

At the same time, Mr. Shealy was giving Gordon the same information. Nannie began telling Lanlad that it was some teenagers who had kidnapped the Courtneys tonight and taken them to Mr. Jasper's shooting house. They drilled them with some questions, and it appeared that a fire was accidentally set when a couple of the boys were tussling around. Patrolman

Shealy happened to be close by and carried the girls out just in time and even his arm received some burns by some of the flames when a rafter had fallen on him, which he protected from the girls. Nannie had applied some burn medicine to his arm and wrapped some gauze on it.

Lanlad asked, "Where are the girls now? They're upstairs getting cleaned up."

Lanlad instantly ran outside and grabbed Shealy with both hands by the front of his collar.

"Why would you have been in the woods at Jasper's shooting house at this time in the morning?" Gordon quickly got in the middle of the two men and said to Lanlad, "It's okay, Mr. Hargis. He confessed everything to me."

Lanlad finally released Shealy's collar and stepped back. "Mr. Hargis, please, please let me explain. First of all, I'm extremely sorry for what happened tonight and also for ever getting involved with any of this."

Mike continued telling them what his involvement had been with the gang.

"I was giving out information from my position at the police station, which would assist the gang in various illegal activities. I was enjoying the benefits I was receiving way too much to care about anyone suffering or getting hurt by my actions. However, things were dangerously escalating and getting completely out of control, and I didn't want to have any part of it anymore. I was riding around all night in the patrol car, trying to figure out how I could walk away from being involved.

On many occasions, I would go to Jasper's shooting house to get some alone time to think or just to get away. As I got closer to the shooting house, I found a couple of parked vehicles. I turned my service vehicle off and I saw a light through the side window of the shack and sat and watched for a moment. I decided to step out to see what was going on inside. I quietly walked to the little house, peered through the window, and saw two young girls tied up. I recognized them from Ice Cream Charlie's when I was there the other night. I remember at one of the gang meetings; Max had discussed there had to be something done to the 'two little snoops,' as he put it, that were causing so much trouble. He talked about terrifying the girls in a way that would make them stop interfering, but I never thought Max would go this far as to kidnap them.

I watched Max as he was attempting to frighten and intimidate them, but I couldn't hear exactly what he was saying. I could see, however, that the girls were pretty shaken up. To the left of the room, two of the boys were scrapping with each other and accidentally knocked over a kerosene lamp. That's how the fire started. Everyone inside ran outside to get away from the fire and, got in the two vehicles and drove away. The fire grew incredibly quickly. I ran around to the front of the house and went inside to untie the girls. I found them both unconscious and also saw a body lying on the floor next to them. I couldn't tell who it was because he was face down. I struggled to get the ropes untied because of the lack of visibility but, thankfully was finally able to untie the girls and carry them out. I went back toward the house to grab the other person, but the fire had gotten so extreme that the front porch had caved in, making it impossible to get inside the shack. I couldn't save whoever was in there."

At this time, only the Courtneys knew that Robby Barton was the person that got killed in the fire trying to save them.

They all went inside and gathered in the den. The Courtneys were visibly shaken but feeling better. Patrolman Shealy began shedding light on the whole situation.

"When I enrolled at the police academy, I was all gung-ho and ready to clean up the whole world of every criminal I could find. After my first year, though, I realized the law enforcement world wasn't as pure and innocent as I had envisioned it. I was introduced to corruption even in those earlier years. Drugs, grades for money, you name it. I tried to ignore it and continue despite it being so abundant. Finally, I graduated with honors, the third highest grade point average, I might add. I got out and came to Henderson and began what I thought would be a great future in a great vocation. My first two years were terrific. There was still more corruption in the force than I wanted to believe, but by this time, I had made myself believe that it was just some of the vocational hazards. I took my first Sergeant's exam and aced it. When the results came out, others were given the promotion who I knew for sure had cheated and suspected even paid off the testing supervisors. I guess that was the beginning of my ending, so to speak."

Shealy's audience continued to listen with compassion yet was careful to keep perspective.

"I tried to get over that disappointment, but after taking the Sergeant's exam two more times and the same thing happening, it made my disappointment and anger more difficult to manage. In fact, it made me very vulnerable for what was about to happen."

"What was that?" Gordon asked.

"One morning about nine months back, Police Chief Moses called me into his office after roll call. Said they were looking for a patrolman who might be interested in doing some undercover work. I thought to myself, this is exactly what I'd been looking for. Maybe this was the chance to prove to the right authorities that I was worthy of getting a promotion. The job was fairly easy. All I had to do was make several buys from a local dealer while they videotaped the transactions. They went off without a hitch! After the bust, we were looking through the dealer's room for other evidence, I found some money hidden away. It was about $6500.00, more money than I'd ever seen at one time. More money than I make in two months. I don't know what happened to me. I guess I justified my action for never getting promoted. I stuffed the money inside my jacket and put it in my locker when I got back to the station. No one saw me, or that's what I thought."

Lanlad inquired, "Well, did someone see you?" "Yessir, but I didn't know it at the time."

"When did you find out?" Coco asked.

Nannie gave her a strict look and said, "Shh!"

Shealy continued. "Well, about a week later, I opened my locker and found a note where the money had been stashed, and it read, 'Don't you hate it when someone knows your dirty little secrets?' Every now and then, I would get a call, and someone on the other end would say, 'I know what you did, and I got the proof.' I was a basket case. Someone was playing games with me, and I didn't know what to do."

He paused for a few seconds to gather his thoughts and continued.

"About two weeks later, Detective Lance Brock asked me to go to lunch with him. I thought that was a little unusual, but then I thought maybe he had an inside track on a detective position that I could apply for. You know, get a head start on everybody else. I was completely off track, though. He started off the conversation with, 'Ain't it great having extra money around?' I asked him what he meant, and he answered, 'Oh, you know. Having a little extra that you can grab from time to time. Like $6500.00'. I was getting real nervous wondering what he was leading up to. That's when he dropped the bomb! He said, 'Look, Shealy, I'm tired of the game. I saw you take the money from that dealer's place. In fact, I have a video on my cell phone of you stuffing it into your pocket. If you don't want the whole city finding out that you're not as clean as you look, then you need to listen up.' I told him I'd give him what's left if he just wouldn't rat me out. He let out one of the evilest laughs I'd ever heard and said, 'Yeah, right! That's chump change, man. I make more than that in a week.' I knew he wasn't talking about his detective salary. He went on to say, 'The way I see it, Shealy, you're pretty much mine.' I asked him what he meant, and he replied, 'You don't get it, yet do you? Look, stupid! Let me lay it out for you. Whatever I need you to do or be or say, that's what you'll do or be or say unless you want me to go to the chief and tell him what I know. Shealy, I might even reward you every now and then if you give me valuable information.' He didn't lie about the rewarding me, part. There's been a couple of times when he's given me $1000.00 for some information. That's when I started calling Brock and telling him anything I thought was newsworthy."

By this time, as interesting as the story was, patience was wearing thin. Gordon asked Patrolman Shealy, "So how does all this play out?"

"Well, Lance has a pretty strong network working, which includes drugs, robberies, vandalism, and other things. The worst thing is he's using a bunch of teenage boys to front his dirty work. The only boy that know he's in charge is a kid named Max and another one named Robby. They are the leaders of this gang that abducted your girls tonight."

"What about other police? Are they involved?" Nannie asked.

"I don't know if there are any other law enforcement people involved or not. It sure wouldn't surprise me."

"What about Chief Moses? You think he's got something to do with all this?" Gordon asked.

"I don't know. At times, he acts pretty strange, but I just don't know."

"Well, Gordon, what do you think we should do?" Lanlad asked.

Shealy jumped in before Gordon could answer and said, "All I can tell you is that you need to be careful. They have everything pretty tight. I mean, you could turn me in, but the evidence I've got wouldn't even hold them for a day. It's my word against a detective's, and that doesn't go very far."

"You sound like you're on our side now!" Nannie chimed in.

"Well, I'd sure like to be. I'd like to try and rectify all the wrong I've done if I had the chance."

"I'm still a little skeptical. Lanlad asked Shealy, What about tonight? That should be some pretty strong evidence, wouldn't it?"

"Yes sir, Mr. Hargis, you'd think so, but it's still my word against Detective Brock's. If someone had been with me and seen what I saw, then that would have made for a much stronger defense."

Nannie shared her thoughts. "What about the girls and what they've seen and what has happened to them? There has to be something we can do or someone we can call."

Gordon broke in, "There's not anyone we can trust right now. This might go deeper than we know. I think I have an idea, though, that will work, but it's pretty extreme."

"What's that, Gordon?" Lanlad asked.

"Well, Max and the gang probably think that your granddaughter and the other Courtney burned up in the fire tonight, right?"

"Oh, what a terrible thought, but I guess you're right," Nannie exclaimed.

Gordon agreed and then continued, "We could use this to our advantage. Now, Shealy, you'd be a key player in this scenario. It would take some stellar acting on your part." "Listen, anything I can do to put Detective Brock and his hoodlums away, I'd be more than willing to do. I know that I'll be indicting myself along with them, but I've got to clear my conscience and make some things right!"

The tension in the room had dropped considerably. Nannie and the girls went into the kitchen to make refreshments. Gordon just received a call about some kind of hunting issue. This allowed Lanlad to get to know more about Shealy. His intentions were to eventually talk to him about Jesus' love and grace. Shealy opened up, telling Lanlad how he'd been brought up in a broken home. His dad just walked out one day when he and his brothers were teenagers and they never heard from him again. Shealy was the middle child of three boys, all two years apart and they seemed to always be in some kind of mischief. His oldest brother was currently serving time for a robbery he committed at a drug store a few years back. His younger brother was still at home since he couldn't keep a job for more than two weeks because of his temper problems. Once Shealy stopped talking, he put his head in his hands and sat with hopelessness. Lanlad got up and sat beside him.

He started sharing with him how Jesus could take his life and give him purpose and meaning. Shealy listened intently. He was very familiar with the scriptures. He went to church when he was a child, but when his daddy left, their mom couldn't keep any of the boys going because she was always working, trying to make ends meet, and didn't have time to go to church either. The boys had gotten incredibly rebellious and were doing their own thing. I was diligent in keeping up my grades and enrolled into college. I followed my career hopes, but my personal life was in shambles. Shealy told Lanlad that he was incredibly embarrassed about the current way he's been living. He said he didn't think God would forgive him for all the wrongs he'd done. Lanlad assured him that everyone is a sinner, and none are too far that the Lord can't save. Shealy began to tear up. Lanlad explained to Shealy how God has been waiting for him to come to Him all these years. He told him he just needed to pray and ask the Lord for forgiveness and ask Jesus to be the Lord of his life. Patrolman Mike Shealy bowed his head and through his tearful voice, asked Jesus to come into his life and change him into the Godly man he needs to be. Gordon had gotten off the phone, and Nannie and the girls were walking in just as Shealy was finishing his prayer. They all gathered around him, hugged him, and praised the Lord for the work He had just done in Patrolman Shealy's life.

After the excitement of Mike receiving Christ into his life, Gordon continued with the plan. "Well, since the boys think the girls died in the fire, as I said earlier, let's use that to our advantage. Shealy, you need to get on the phone and call Detective Brock. See if he knows what happened this morning. Whether he's heard about it or not, tell him you're extremely scared, and you're going to the authorities."

"Oh, I think I know where you're headed. He'll try to calm me down and probably ask me to meet him somewhere so we can talk about it. Most likely, he'll try and pay me off. It might even get more serious that."

"Yeah, there's that possibility, for sure," Gordon said regretfully.

Shealy said, "I'd be crazy to like the thought of dying, but I think this plan is the best chance we got."

CHAPTER SIX: DETECTIVE BROCK AND THE STING

Nannie and Lanlad had prayer with the Courtneys and told them to go to bed. Of course, they didn't want to and whined quite a bit, but to no avail. Once the girls got their pajamas on and into their beds, they decided to pray for protection and safety for Patrolman Shealy and Gordon. Also, the plan they devised would go smoothly.

Mike called Detective Brock at his home. It was 4:15, and Shealy knew he wouldn't be excited to be awakened by a call from him at that time in the morning. Brock answered the phone and let out some crude obscenities.

Brock said, "What are you calling me at 4:30 in the morning? Are you crazy?"

"No, but I am pretty nervous that we might have a big problem."

Shealy sounded extremely convincing.

"What kind of problem?"

"Then you don't know, do you?"

"Quit playing games with me, Shealy. What's the problem?" Shealy proceeded to tell him what had occurred during the most recent morning hours and the tragic death of the girls and whoever the other person was in the shack that died in the fire. Sure enough, Brock hadn't heard about any of this. Shealy went on to detail the recent events. At the end, he tacked on that he was going to the authorities. That he couldn't take it anymore, and he didn't care how good the money was. He told Lance he didn't want any part of this mess any longer!"

Brock sat up in his bed and began to sound a little uneasy. "Now, listen, Shealy. There's nothing to worry your little head about. This can never be traced back to us. We had nothing to do with it."

"Yeah, I know, but we've had everything else to do with the things those boys have been involved in. I didn't like being involved with the bank robbery or the other houses being broken in. And I especially didn't like Barton's own son stealing money from his dad's grocery store. But this earlier tonight, this has gone too far."

Lance quickly shot back, "Well, you sure enjoyed taking home the benefits, though, didn't cha?"

There was a long hesitation, then Brock spoke again.

"Look, Mike, you're overreacting. If it ever came out, it would be our word against some bunch of young punk teenager's words. Who do you think would win out?"

Shealy thought to himself, "This man would sell out his own mother if it meant saving his own hide!"

Brock's plan was beginning to unfold just as Gordon and Shealy had hoped. Trying to calm Shealy down, he said, "Look, let's meet over at the cotton gin warehouse. I'll meet you there in an hour and a half."

The cotton gin had been closed for years, and no one ever went there anymore. Occasionally, the police would have to clear out a teenage party or two that would get out of hand, but that was it. The gin was a perfect place for Brock because no one would be there.

"Alright, I'll see you there." Shealy had seemingly pulled it off. That was the easy part, though. Now, he had to take precautions to make sure he doesn't get killed. He and Gordon discussed as many details as they could think of to keep any potential danger to a minimum. Shealy said, "I have a recording device in my truck. I'll wear it and get as much information as I can when we meet. Gordon, let's pray and ask God's help in all this." Gordon agreed. They got Nannie and Lanlad together, and all four held hands and prayed for God's guidance.

Detective Lance Brock immediately called Max and confirmed Patrolman Shealy's information.

"This time, you let things get way out of hand. What were you thinking, you idiot? Everything else up to this point has gone just as I planned, and then you had to muddle it up. Shealy is claiming that he's going to the authorities, so I'm gonna have to give him more money to keep his mouth shut. I hope I don't have to kill the punk."

"Sorry, boss. We were just sick and tired of those little brats and thought we'd put a little scare into them. We didn't think it'd turn out the way it did."

"Yeah, well, you won't have to worry about them anymore now that they're dead, will ya? Who was the other person they found dead?"

With a slight hesitation in his voice, Max answered, "Robby."

Brock said louder than he meant to, "Robby Barton?"

"Yessir."

"How did that happen?"

"I'm not sure, but as everyone was leaving, I think he went back into the house to get the girls out. I don't know if the fire got him or the smoke. Probably the smoke since he had such bad asthma issues."

"Well, I hope you're really proud of yourself for all the problems you've caused. Such an idiot! You do realize that he's dead because of you. Now, look. I've worked out a plan to meet with Shealy this morning at the old cotton gin. You get your tail out there right now, and make sure you park your car out of sight. There's an office that overlooks the whole compound. Find it and get in it! Be sure to take that small automatic I gave you, just in case you need it. Once you get there, stay out of sight. If everything goes as planned, I'll see you later at the convenience store. Understand?"

"Yessir," Max responded.

They hung up, and Detective Brock went to work. He thought of many different ways to make Shealy's death look convincing and believable enough. Perhaps he could make it look like a suicide. Maybe he could make it look like he stumbled upon a drug transaction, and some drug dealer shot him. No, he thought. That would be too heroic. He thought sarcastically to himself; so many prospects and such little time. After giving the idea a little more time, he finally decided that he liked the scenario of Shealy stumbling upon a drug transaction. He just happened to have some cocaine for such occasions as this. He consented within himself and considered the least he could do for a guy who had assisted in the gang's criminal activities was to let him die a hero. He chuckled to himself and thought, "Brock, you're brilliant!"

Max slipped out of the house without his parents waking up. He left a note saying that he and Robby were going fishing. That alibi always seemed to work, and Robby and he really did do a lot of fishing in the summertime. He pushed his car out of the driveway. It was a good thing for him that it was on a slight hill. Once he coasted far enough away, he started the engine and drove toward the cotton gin. Once there, he found a perfect place to park. He then climbed up the stairs that went to the old, abandoned office Brock told him about. The door was opened about six inches. He was able to move the debris behind it, which kept it from opening all the way. Out came a couple of rats and scared Max to death. He jumped and danced all around the office. After a thorough investigation to make sure there weren't any other rats or other creatures in the office, he finally settled in and found a place to sit. He was perched high enough to see just about anything that could happen. He thought to himself that he might come here more often. He liked the feeling of being up high and alone in this office. Yeah, it will become his own little office in the sky. He laughed a little under his breath.

Gordon and Shealy's prayer time was short and to the point. They tested the recording device to make sure it was recording properly, and it worked perfectly. They got into Shealy's car and were about a mile away from the gin when Gordon said, "Shealy, stop the car and let me get into the trunk."

He stopped the vehicle and popped the trunk. Gordon climbed in and, held up the trunk with his hand, and looked at Patrolman Shealy.

"Hey. Be careful and don't try and be a hero out there. I'll be watching and if I see anything that I think looks suspicious, I'll let you know real quickly. Hey, who knows? Maybe Brock will try and work some kind of a deal with you."

"I don't know. Gordon. I got a funny feeling he'd rather just get me out of the way. Do you mind if we say another quick prayer?"

It really amazed Gordon that Shealy was so sensitive to the Lord and trusted Him in this situation. Gordon said that would be a great idea and said a short prayer.

"Father, Shealy, and I are about to get into something we're not really sure about, but we pray for Your guidance and wisdom. We also pray for Your protection. Thank You, Lord, for who You are and that You are worthy of our trust. We love You!"

"Thanks, man! I know God is gonna take care of us!" Shealy said with an impressive new-found faith.

Brock had already arrived and had parked his car. He was getting out of his when Max saw him and ran down the stairwell to talk to him. Max yelled at him on his way down. It startled Brock so much that he quickly pulled out his pistol and drew down on Max. Max stopped dead in his tracks and held up his hands.

"Whoa, boss. It's just me."

"Are you stupid? I told you to stay out of sight."

"Yeah, I know, but I was just gonna tell you I found the office."

After Brock spouted out some choice words, he whispered as loudly as he could, "Just get your hind end back up there, and fast. And keep your eyes peeled."

"Yeah, yeah, okay. Sorry, boss."

Max ran back up the stairs just in time. Shealy was pulling around the corner of the warehouse, and he saw Brock standing beside his car with his arms folded and one of his patented grins on his face. As he pulled up closer, Shealy thought back to all the criminal activities he had been an accessory to over the past eight months. How stupid he had been to think that money, stolen money at that, would bring happiness and contentment.

A couple of verses of scripture from his past surprisingly came to his memory, "Be sure your sins will find you out" and "You reap what you sow!"

He thought to himself, "Have those ever proven to be true?" He whispered another prayer.

Gordon opened the trunk just enough to see out. Shealy had made sure that he parked the car at an angle where Gordon would be able to see and not be seen. As he opened his door, he whispered to Gordon, "Well, here goes."

Gordon wished he could talk back to him for encouragement, but the wire was only one way, and it was recording everything. Brock was walking toward Shealy's car to meet Shealy. Shealy got out, and Brock greeted him like an old friend he hadn't seen in years.

"Hello, Mike. Good to see you! Now, what is this about you wanting to go to the authorities? You're just trying to pull a joke on me, right?"

"No, Lance, I'm not. This is no joke. I can't go on living with myself with the knowledge about all the wrong things I've done and that I've been involved in. Robberies and break-ins are one thing, but children dying is another."

"Look, Mike, you're just scared right now. I'm just as sorry as you are about those kids, but sometimes there is collateral damage. It's not our fault. You're not thinking clearly. Let's go back to my place, and we'll booze it up a little, and things will begin to clear up."

"No, Lance. I ain't kidding. I'm taking you in with me, and I'm gonna tell everything to the authorities."

"Okay, I tell you what. Keep your mouth shut, and I'll put another five grand into your Canadian account."

"Brock, you just don't get it. I'm quitting and taking you and everyone involved down with me."

Brock casually turned in the opposite direction, and before Shealy could pull out his gun, Brock beat him to the punch.

"I don't think so. Shealy. You have been very good to have around these past few months, very helpful with all the information and intel you've given, but if you're this serious about going straight, I guess I gotta get rid of you before you mess everything up. You're no use to me anymore."

"Brock, you know you won't get away with killing me."

Brock let out an evil, demonic-sounding laugh and said, "Shealy, you're so stupid. All I'll have to do is say you got a tip from an informant that a drug deal was going down at the cotton gin. You came out here without any backup, and the dealer apparently shot and killed you."

Max, watching as carefully as a cat would watch a mouse, noticed a slight upward movement of Shealy's trunk. Gordon had lifted it up a little higher after he'd heard Brock's last statement he made to Shealy. Max was holding his small automatic in his hand and jumped up to warn Brock. He began running down the stairs, and he was only two or three steps from hitting the ground when he tripped. His finger accidentally pulled the trigger, and the revolver went off. For a brief moment, Brock looked away to see where it came from. That gave Shealy just enough time to knock Brock's .357 out of his hand and onto the ground. Brock turned around and started running away. At the same time, Gordon jumped out of the trunk to give Shealy some reinforcement. Brock never saw Gordon coming. He tackled him, and Shealy came right behind, holding Brock's own gun.

"You're so stupid, Shealy. Don't you know when you turn me in, you're going down, too?"

"Yeah, Brock, I'm counting on it. I don't know how much time I'm gonna have to spend behind bars, maybe the rest of my life, but I gotta make things right."

"You're a fool, Shealy!"

"No, Brock. A fool is one who is so blind he can't even see the hole he's falling into."

"Shut up, Shealy! You're making me sick!" Lance Brock said with contempt.

Gordon asked Shealy why Detective shot his pistol. Shealy answered and said it wasn't him.

Max had had ample time to go around to the other side of the warehouse and sneak up behind Shealy and Gordon.

"Yo! Drop the gun, Shealy!" Max said. When Shealy turned around to see who it was, Brock saw an opportunity to return the favor to Shealy that he had done to him earlier. He kicked his own gun out of Shealy's hand. He and Brock went into a scuffle while Gordon went for the gun. Max got trigger-happy and shot a couple of shots toward Gordon.

"Ahh!" He was hit! One of Max's potshots found a home in Gordon's left thigh. Gordon dropped to the ground, grimacing in pain. Brock was able to catch Shealy with his right hand down and threw a jab under his chin. It freed Brock enough to run over to where his gun was and pick it up.

"Max, remind me to give you a little extra this week. Now for you two scums, what am I gonna do with you?"

"Look, Brock," Shealy began. Do what you have to me, but don't mess with the game warden. He only came to help me. He doesn't know much of anything."

"Sure, oh, okay. There, Mr. Game Warden, you're free to go. See ya!" Brock said facetiously.

"I mean, really, Shealy, tell me something. Do I really look that stupid to you? Max, go get their car and bring it over here."

Max went to get the car while Brock proceeded to tell them their fate.

"Well, let's see now. This is working out better than I expected. I can see it in the headlines right now, 'Game warden and Patrolman are caught in a sting operation by Detective Brock. Both were caught in the middle of a drug transaction. Detective Brock had suspected them for quite a while. Detective Brock was not able to apprehend those who were actually selling the drugs.'"

As Max was walking back into the old gin, Brock looked at him and said, "Yeah, the story sounds pretty convincing, doesn't it, Max?"

"Yeah, pretty smart, boss."

Gordon asked, "And how will you explain the .38 bullet in my leg when you have a .357?"

"Ask me harder one next time! One of the guys you were selling to was shooting at me, and they accidentally hit you!"

Shealy said, "Give it up, Brock. It's all too lame. You'll never get away with it."

"You've been watching too many old movies, Shealy. This is 2010. The good guy never wins anymore. You know what, Shealy? I was gonna let you die a hero. I was gonna say that some snitch called me and told me you were up here dead. That some drug dealer you were trying to bust killed you. But since you brought your little buddie along, I'm forced to use this other story. What a shame! Just think, you could have died a hero. Now you're gonna rot in prison."

Gordon and Patrolman Shealy looked at each other and only shook their heads. Things weren't turning out nearly like they thought they should.

"Max, keep them covered while I look around and make sure there isn't anything I'm missing to mess up my story. Don't take your eyes off them for one second. If they try anything, go ahead and shoot 'em. We have the story that will cover your .38 if you do have to use it."

Brock took a short walk around the compound. He wanted to make sure everything would fall into place when the scene was investigated. As soon as he was out of hearing distance, Mike Shealy thought he'd try talking some sense into Max. He prayed and asked the Lord to soften his heart. "Max?"

Max didn't answer. He acted as if he didn't even hear Shealy.

He continued, "You know you're in a lot of trouble, and this is only going to compound it. If you were to let us go right now and help us take Brock in, that would go a long way with the judge."

"Shut up! Just shut up!"

Gordon chimed in, "Look, Max. You can't go on this way. There's always a payday."

Max shoved the gun into Gordon's face and said, "Look! I said to shut up, and I mean it! I'm going places, and Brock's the man that's gonna help me get there."

"The only place Brock is gonna take you is prison." Max slapped his pistol across Gordon's face to shut him up.

"Listen to Gordon," Shealy said compassionately.

"Yeah, listen, Max," said Brock as he came around the corner.

"These two combined make about $70,000 to $80,000 a year. We can make that in about six months. Yeah, you be sure to listen."

Shealy looked at Brock and said, "Brock, I really feel sorry for you and only for what you can get. You're living only for yourself."

"Hey, man, that's the American way, right, Max?"

Both Max and Brock broke into laughter. Then Brock got serious again and, after handcuffing each of them, said, "Come on, you two. Get in the car. It's time we play out this little charade down at the station."

As he shoved Shealy, he felt something unusual on Shealy's back. He jerked his shirt up and found the wire and recorder.

"Well, ain't this just perfect?"

"You know, somebody upstairs must really love me."

"What is it, boss?" Max asked.

"Oh, it's just a little, oh, recorder that could implicate us for everything we've been doing. Thank you, Shealy, I'll take this!"

And with a rip, he tore the tape off his back, which was holding the recorder in place. He put it into his pocket and shoved Shealy into the backseat.

CHAPTER SEVEN: T. K. ADAMS

The Hargis were pretty worried, to say the least. It was already 7:15 that morning, and they hadn't heard from either Gordon or Patrolman Shealy. They heard the girls coming down the stairs.

"What are you two doing up so early? You've only been to bed for a couple of hours," Nannie asked.

Coco answered that they had both just woken up. They asked if anything more had happened. Nannie commented that they hadn't heard from Gordon or Shealy since they left to meet Detective Brock. She told them Lanlad had decided to take a drive to the cotton gin to see if he might spot something out of the ordinary. Coco asked if she and Courtney could go with him.

"Well, I guess it'd be okay. I'm just gonna ride by to see if I can see anything. Come on."

Nannie interjected, "I think I'll come along, too." They all piled into their suburban and headed down Hwy. 17, which was the old country highway that passed right by the old cotton gin building. They were about three miles from the old gin when Detective Brock drove passed them with Max driving right behind him. Coco recognized Gordon and Shealy sitting in the back of Shealy's car like common criminals. Lanlad slowed down enough to make a U-turn and proceeded to follow them in the same direction that they were going.

Courtney asked Lanlad, "Where do you think they're going."

"I don't know, but I don't have a good feeling about it."

As they continued, they saw them pull directly into the parking lot of the Police station. Lanlad was able to park across the street in the grocery parking lot. They watched in horror as Detective Brock jerked them out of the car, both handcuffed and shoved them along into the station's front doors. Lanlad's first inclination was to drive over there and help, but the problem was he didn't know how to help. This was a really confusing turn of events. Totally unexpected! It was supposed to be Patrolman Shealy and Gordon bringing Brock in, not the other way around.

Coco said, "Let's go to the station and tell them what we know, Lanlad."

"We have to wait and see what's gonna happen next. It appears that Brock has turned the table somehow, and we have to be very careful not to fall into the same apparent trap that Gordon and Mike have."

All eyes turned as the three of them busted through the doors. "Sergeant Harmon, book these two for the sell and distribution of narcotics."

"What?" Desk Sergeant Harmon asked in surprise. He recognized Patrolman Shealy right off but didn't know Gordon.

"I said book these two."

Brock was starting to unravel his devious plan.

"I've been watching them for a long time, and I finally nailed them. Caught them right in the act. Oh, yeah, and get this one some medical assistance. He caught a bullet in the leg."

Harmon never liked Brock; in fact, few did. He was quite a hotdog. Always looking out for number one. Gordon was able to get his leg patched up and both of them were placed into the city jail and, of course, both suspended until further notice. They were able to make bail within the hour. Now, what would they do? How would they get out of this? Where would they start? They got in Patrolman Shealy's personal car and were going to drive back to the Hargis' house.

"Gordon, I'm so sorry that I got you involved in this mess."

"Mike, no apology necessary. I really believe God works in all situations, and I know He's going to work this situation out somehow."

Gordon noticed Lanlad waving him to come over to the parking lot across from the police station. They did and Lanlad asked them what happened. Mike and Gordon told them they would give them the full story at their home. Once at the Hargis' house, they explained the unfortunate incident and how it played out for them. Coco said, "Why don't we go back to the gin and do some investigating? We might find something that would help their case."

Lanlad said, "That's not a bad idea. What do you think, Nannie?"

Nannie responded, "Well, do you think it would be safe enough for us all to be there?"

Shealy answered, "It should be. Since there wasn't any murder, there wouldn't be any investigation going on."

"Can we go, please, please?"

Both Courtneys spoke in unison.

"I guess so, but you two are going to have to stay close to me," Nannie said.

They all piled into the Hargis' van and drove for the cotton gin. When they arrived, everyone split up in different directions. Gordon headed inside the warehouse, and Shealy and Lanlad stayed outside where the cars had been parked. Nannie and the girls walked around the sides of the old building. Gordon looked up before he went inside and noticed a couple of opened windows. Inside, he saw the stairs and started up. He was just about halfway up, and something brass caught his eye. He went back down and picked it up. It was a shell from a small automatic pistol lying on the ground. He put it in his pocket and went back upstairs. He thought this apparently was Max's position during the altercation. He figured that's how Max saw him climb out of the trunk and it probably was his pistol that they heard while at the gin earlier. There wasn't any other noticeable evidence, so he walked down and looked through the warehouse. As Nannie and the girls were outside walking around the building, they accidentally flushed out a rabbit from some underbrush. It jumped up and took off running. They thought they would die. They finally settled down and continued their search for some evidence. Lanlad and Shealy searched diligently for anything that might give them a lead, and they, too, were coming up completely dry.

Then they heard Gordon yell for them to come inside. They and Nannie and the girls ran inside and found him and another gentleman standing there with him. He was an older man in his late fifties, pretty gruff-looking, unshaven, terribly wrinkled clothes and a backpack sitting on the ground alongside him. Gordon began, "Let me introduce to you, T. K. Adams, a very important man!"

They all greeted him with a certain curious cordiality, and he returned the same. Gordon then proceeded to tell them why he was so important.

"T. K. is a fellow who likes to travel and isn't really tied to anyone or anywhere. T. K.? Do you mind telling them your story?"

"No, not at all. You see, I'm the type that don't like to settle down nowhere. I don't hurt nobody, and I don't bum off nobody, either. I work when I need to, and I work really hard. I ain't no moocher and don't look for any handouts. Usually, I like to keep to myself and keep my life very simple, but this morning, I saw some things go on that I can't just let go by without doing something about it."

Gordon jumped in when T. K. took a breath. "That's why I said he's so important. He saw everything that happened this morning."

"You mean he saw what happened between you two and Brock?" Lanlad inquired.

"Not only saw it, but I also heard it all, too. I got a great hearing. My granddaddy told me to take care of my ears, and they'll take care of you."

T. K. went on to tell a story of how he had fallen asleep on some train tracks once, and he heard the train just in time, thanks to his ears.

"T. K, are you willing to stand before a jury and tell what you saw and heard this morning?" Patrolman Shealy asked.

"Let me answer that this way. You see, somewhere, I've got a couple of grandchildren. I've only seen 'em once. You see, my past ain't the best. Done some wrong things with some business deals, and I used to drink way too much alcohol, which got me in a lot of trouble. My son didn't want me negatively influencing his two beautiful girls, and he asked me not to come around until I got my life together. That's been quite a few years now. He sighed a little and continued. Well, anyway, Gordon, here, tells me that these two young girls are possibly in some trouble, and something has gotta be done about this Detective Brock feller. If me telling all I've seen today to a judge and jury will help put that scoundrel away, then I'll do anything I can."

"T. K., how 'bout you coming to our house for dinner tonight?" Nannie asked while looking at Lanlad at the same time to make sure he was okay with that.

Lanlad nodded and agreed and said, "We'd love to have you."

"Well, as I said earlier, I ain't no moocher and-"

Nannie broke in and said, "You're not mooching when you're invited. We're having roast beef, potato casserole, green beans, hot buttery rolls, and for dessert, I made a pecan pie."

"Well, since you put it that way, I reckon I'd love to come."

They all climbed into the van, and it was pretty plain that T. K. hadn't had a bath in a while. On the way to the Hargis' house, Gordon was reminded about what he'd found earlier.

"Oh, by the way, I found something else. I found a shell from a small automatic pistol. I think it's from Max's pistol."

"Yeah, I think you're right. It looks like the Lord has shined down upon us with us meeting up with T. K. and you finding that shell. He sure is good, isn't He?"

Visibly disturbed, T. K. snapped, "No, He ain't! And I'm surprised to hear a grown man say such a thing!"

Statements like that never seemed to bother Lanlad. He would just use them as an opportunity to talk to that person about the Lord.

"Why, T. K., sounds like you've had a couple of bad experiences," Lanlad spoke.

"You dang straight, I have. I used to go to church real regularly, my whole family and me. That was until our preacher took off with about $95,000 of the church's money. We'd been taking up a special offering to build a church for a missionary in Brazil. It took about 10 months to raise that much and he up and stole it!"

"That is terrible, T. K," Nannie commented.

"Not only that, but the new preacher we got after him was just as bad. He was the most two-faced person I'd ever met. He'd lie to you right in front of your face. He was really good at playing up to the people who had money in the church just to get them to help him out when he wanted something. Plain pathetic! I tell you, if I don't ever see another preacher again, it'd be too soon for me."

Lanlad wanted to talk to him about Jesus but felt like he better wait until the time was better. That's when Coco, in her tactless way, said, "T. K., I don't think you should let those preachers or any other preachers keep you from Jesus. He didn't do any of that stuff. They did, and they'll have to answer for that themselves. Our Sunday Bible teacher told our class one Sunday that someone can't blame Mozart just because someone played his music badly."

No one knew what to say, nor did they know what T. K.'s response would be. T. K. just sat there. That's when Courtney spoke up and said, "T. K., I think I know how you feel. One time I was in Sunday school, and a couple of girls were laughing the whole time. I didn't know why until a friend of mine told me. They were laughing at my hair. They were making fun of how it looked. I didn't want to ever go back to church, but my mom told me something."

By this time, T. K. had some tears beginning to form in his eyes.

Courtney continued. "Mom told me that it didn't matter what anyone says or does to us. The most important thing to remember is that Jesus loves us so much that He died for us, and that's the reason that we should keep going to church and serving the Lord."

T. K. was clearly shaken by what the Courtneys had said. Children sometimes have a way of getting through to adults when adults can't. There wasn't any conversation for the rest of the way to the Hargis' home. As they walked up to the house, Lanlad put his arm around T. K. and asked him if he wanted to get a little cleaned up. T. K. nodded, and Lanlad showed him where the bathroom was and also had some clothes that might fit him.

"I want you to have these clothes, and I don't want to hear anything about you mooching them off me; you here?" Lanlad said with a big grin on his face.

T. K. looked up and told Lanlad, "I really do appreciate all this. You all are some of the nicest people I've met in a long time."

About that time, Nannie yelled that supper would be ready in about forty-five minutes.

"Go on and get cleaned up, and we'll talk later," Lanlad said to T. K.

The girls stayed outside a little longer and rode their bikes while Shealy and Lanlad discussed what their next move should be. Gordon called Lori, at Nannie's request, and invited her over to eat with them and get caught up on everything that had happened.

After he called Lori, he joined Lanlad and Shealy in their discussion. Shealy looked at Gordon and said, "What do you think about this idea? Lanlad and I thought we'd take a chance and go to Police Chief Moses and confide in him. We have to trust somebody, and Moses seems to be the most likely candidate."

"Yeah, I'd have to agree," Lanlad said.

"I know people can fool you, but you can just see that some people are okay, and I think Moses might be one of those people. A little crude and sometimes rude, but a genuine kind of person."

By that time, T. K. had walked into the room. He looked and smelled like a million bucks. His face was completely shaved, and his hair had a natural wave. He actually was quite handsome.

"My, my, my! T. K. You look mighty handsome for an old man," Lanlad said with a chuckle. T. K., a little embarrassed, bypassed the compliment and got right into their discussion.

"Who's this Moses character?"

After they explained to him who he was and a couple of other details about him he said, "Why don't you get him over here and let's have a talk and see what happens?"

They all sat down and enjoyed another one of Nannie's unbelievable suppers. While rubbing his stomach, T. K. said, "Whew, I haven't eaten like that in years, Mrs. Hargis. Boy, was it good!"

"Well, thank you, Mr. Adams, I'm glad you enjoyed it."

Recognizing some sarcasm in her voice, T. K. said, "Okay, okay, I'll call you Nannie if you call me T. K., deal?"

"Deal," Nannie replied. Nannie, Lori, and the girls all helped clean the kitchen.

Coco asked, "Why is it that the women always have to do the cleaning up?"

"Yeah, why is that?" Courtney added to the question.

Lori answered before Nannie gave her own wisdom on the subject, "You see, men are incapable of doing much more than changing channels on a television or relaxing in a recliner."

"Ooh, Lori! It's a good thing those men can't hear you."

"Oh, I thought I said it loud enough for them to hear me."

This time Lori repeated it and was plenty loud for all the men to hear. Both Courtneys were howling with laughter.

Shealy said, "Boy, Gordon, you sure have a feisty one in there!"

"Don't I know it?" Gordon agreed.

T. K. was taking all this in little by little. It sure felt good to be around a family again.

Lanlad called Police Chief Moses earlier and asked him if he could come to the house, that he had some news that he might be interested in hearing. By the time Moses arrived, the ladies had finished the dishes, and the men had prepared themselves to meet with the chief. The front doorbell rang, and Lanlad opened their front door. Moses didn't wait for an invitation but walked right past Lanlad and into the den. Everyone greeted him and Nannie asked him to have a seat. He was surprised to find Patrolman Shealy and Gordon there and was wondering who the stranger was.

After nodding his head toward them, he said in his non-diplomatic way, "So, what is this news that was so important for me to drive all the way out here to hear?"

Lanlad started, "Well, we have what we think is strong evidence to prove that Patrolman Shealy and Gordon are innocent."

"Oh, you do? Now, what might that be? Seems to me that Detective Brock's side of the story is airtight."

"May I step in Lanlad?" asked Patrolman Shealy.

"Chief, Brock is involved in things you'd never believe. I wouldn't even believe them if I hadn't been involved in them myself."

"You know that's an incriminating statement, son."

"Yessir, I know and am willing to do more of it to make sure Lance Brock and the others involved get locked up and Gordon is acquitted. I've been involved in too many of the illegal activities for too long that have been going on in Altonville. I have to make things right, even though it means I'll be spending some time in jail. I just want Brock and his group to be stopped. You see, Chief Moses, many of the robberies, fires, vandalism, and other things have been part of a master plan that Brock put together."

"That's a wild accusation if you don't have anything to back it up with, Shealy. What are you getting at?"

Pointing to T. K., Shealy said, "Let me introduce T. K. Adams."

"Shealy, I don't need to meet any new characters. I just need you to hurry up and get to the point?"

"Yessir. Early this morning, I called Brock to tell him I didn't want to have anything else to do with him or his group of hoodlums and misfits and the illegal activity. After these two girls were almost burned to death in Jasper's shooting house last night."

"What? Are these the two girls that were in that fire? How come I wouldn't know about that? I was there, and no one said anything about any children being in the house."

"That's what I'm getting at, Chief. No one knows because we were using it to try and get to Brock."

Turning to the Courtneys, Moses asked, "What were you two doing out there that time of the night, and how did you two wind up in that fire, anyway?"

The Courtneys went through each detail of the early morning event, and for the first time, Moses began to look like he was beginning to believe the stories he was being told.

T. K. interjected, "Chief Moses, I saw and heard this feller Brock and some young kid named Max at the cotton gin, putting the stranglehold on Gordon and Shealy."

As T. K. finished his story, Moses spoke up.

"I guess I can tell you now. I've been suspicious about Brock for about two years now but never had anything strong enough to pin him on. When I'd get close to suspecting something, the situation would change, and Brock would come out smelling like a rose. So, all of the suspicions I had were true, and now, I finally have enough concrete evidence to put him away. Nothing makes me madder than an enforcer of the law being crooked. Getting back to you, Shealy, again, you realize that you're indicting yourself with all these confessions?"

"Like I said before, Chief. I'm not really worried about me; I just want Brock to be put out of commission and Gordon set free. In fact, Chief, unless they've changed their plans, I think Brock has his gang hitting the convenience store tomorrow where Max works."

"What time?"

"It was supposed to be when Max takes the day's receipts to the bank. The one who closes always puts the money in a regular grocery bag to keep down any suspicion. The gang was going to get it from him in the parking lot and make it look like a robbery. It looks like a lot of the illegal activity has been on that same premise."

"What do you mean, Chief?" Gordon asked.

"Well, now that y'all have shed some light on some of this stuff, it would appear that many of the break-ins, if not all of them, are inside jobs. It makes sense why we had such a hard time finding proper evidence. Tomorrow night, we'll set up a sting operation at the convenience store parking lot and catch those rascals red-handed."

As Police Chief Moses was walking out the door, he turned around and said, "By the way, I need you all to come down to the station and give me your statements again so I can get 'em on videotape. And Shealy, there's a possibility that the judge will have some leniency with you since you've made such a change, but there ain't no guarantees?"

Shealy nodded in response as Lanlad told Moses, "Thank you."

That next night, just like Shealy had said, the gang was in the parking lot looking as inconspicuous as they possibly could. Chief Moses had put men inside the store as well as in the parking lot. Max closed the front door and walked toward his car. In his hand was a grocery sack that had approximately $5000.00 in it. It was all on video. A couple of the boys approached Max, and without any struggle, Max handed them the bag. The police made their presence known and apprehended everyone involved except Brock. Where was he?

In the corner of Moses' eye, he noticed a vehicle driving away. He strained a little harder and saw that it was Brock. He took off after him, and when Brock saw the police lights in his rear-view mirror, he tried to speed away. For twenty minutes, Moses and Brock were driving on roads leading out of town at speeds no less than 75 miles an hour. Finally, Moses began to close in on him. Ahead of Brock was a 90-degree turn that a professional racecar driver couldn't have even made. When Brock tried to turn, his car flipped at least three times and then hit a big oak tree. His vehicle landed upside down, with Brock hanging halfway out of the back window. Moses called for an ambulance and jumped out of his car to see if he could help Brock. He knelt down beside him and felt for a pulse, but it was too late.

EPILOGUE

The interrogation was an interesting situation, to say the least. Most of the boys gave more than enough information about all their criminal events, which made it quite easy to get every bit of incriminating evidence the police would need to indict all involved. There weren't any other law enforcement people involved, which was comforting to the city and Chief Moses. It didn't take the jury long to convict the boys of the many felonies they had been involved in. Robberies, arson, vandalism, and even attempted murder.

The judge did, in fact, show leniency to Patrolman Shealy and only sentenced him to ten years. He'd probably be out much sooner. While in prison, Shealy was going to try and start a prison ministry. Lanlad said he'd help any way he could by providing Bibles and time. Another huge thing that happened was that T. K. Adams decided to make things right with the Lord. He even found his son and began building back their lost relationship. His son even allowed him to spend some time with his grandchildren. The Courtneys went back to Ridgeland, Mississippi, and their parents were glad to have them back. Now, they could continue the rest of their summer, where they might just find another adventuresome mystery to get involved in.